WORLD'S EDGE

A MOSAIC NOVEL

JAMES SALLIS

SOHO

Published by
Soho Press, Inc.
227 W 17th Street
New York, NY 10011
www.sohopress.com

Some of the stories in this collection originally appeared, sometimes in slightly different form, in other publications. For a complete list, see p. 227.

Library of Congress Cataloging-in-Publication Data is available.

ISBN 978-1-64129-826-1
eISBN 978-1-64129-827-8

Interior design by Janine Agro, Soho Press, Inc.

Printed in the United States of America

10 9 8 7 6 5 4 3 2 1

EU Responsible Person (for authorities only)
eucomply OÜ
Pärnu mnt 139b-14
11317 Tallinn, Estonia
hello@eucompliancepartner.com
www.eucompliancepartner.com

Praise for James Sallis

"Spellbinding . . . Like a piece of stormy poetry."

—The New York Times

"Slim and affecting . . . Sallis writes of life's mishaps as well as its consolations in a poetic style."

—The Wall Street Journal

"The power of simplicity and the musical ring of truth as only Sallis can deliver it—as he has done bravely, consistently, for the last few decades."

—Los Angeles Times

"One stark and stunning tale of murder, treachery, and deceit . . . Packs a wallop." ***—The Boston Globe***

"A taut page-turner . . . [and] a lovely piece of work that makes you wish some other writers would take lessons from [Sallis]." ***—The Washington Post***

"A lean and nasty piece of neo-noir. I took my seat on page one and didn't get back up again until it ended (far too quickly). Always a pleasure to be in the hands of a master like James Sallis." **—Dennis Lehane**

"James Sallis is one of our greatest living crime writers . . . Try to get his words, his stories, his people out of your head. Just try." **—Laura Lippman**

"Then there's James Sallis—he's right up there, one of the best. It is quite possible that speaking of Jim Sallis in the same tone as Poe and Dostoevsky is not overblowing on my part." **—Harlan Ellison**

"Imagine the heart of Jim Thompson beating in the poetic chest of James Sallis . . . Beauty, sadness and power." ***—Chicago Tribune***

"Sallis is a gifted writer . . . A superbly potent brew that burns going down and explodes in the belly."

—Alfred Hitchcock Mystery Magazine

"James Sallis probably couldn't write a boring line if he tried." ***—The Irish Times***

"James Sallis might be the 'purest' writer of crime fiction in America today . . . His books are worth reading solely for what rises from the inspired use of language." ***—San Francisco Chronicle***

"In addition to his masterly novels, Sallis is known for his work as a poet, and the lyrical beauty of his words shines through his pages . . . It's a crime that a writer this good isn't better known."

—Chicago Sun-Times

WORLD'S EDGE

ALSO BY THE AUTHOR

THE LEW GRIFFIN NOVELS
The Long-Legged Fly
Moth
Black Hornet
Eye of the Cricket
Bluebottle
Ghost of a Flea

THE JOHN TURNER SERIES
Cypress Grove
Cripple Creek
Salt River

THE DRIVER SERIES
Drive
Driven

OTHER NOVELS
Renderings
Death Will Have Your Eyes
The Killer Is Dying
Others of My Kind
Willnot
Sarah Jane

NONFICTION
Difficult Lives: Jim Thompson—David Goodis—Chester Himes
Gently into the Land of the Meateaters
Chester Himes: A Life
The Guitar Players

STORIES
A Few Last Words
Limits of the Sensible World
Time's Hammers: Collected Stories
A City Equal to My Desire
Potato Tree and Other Stories
Dayenu and Other Stories
What You Were Fighting For
Bright Segments: The Complete Collected Short Fiction

POETRY
Sorrow's Kitchen
My Tongue in Other Cheeks: Selected Translations
Rain's Eagerness
Black Night's Gonna Catch Me Here: New and Selected Poems
Night's Pardons
Ain't Long 'Fore Day

AS EDITOR
Ash of Stars: On the Writing of Samuel R. Delany
Jazz Guitars: An Anthology
The Guitar in Jazz

In memory of my brother,
John Sallis

QUICKLY

Define the cadence of rain
in this treetop. Explain
the grass's soft voice.
Give me once more
three reasons for storm.
Describe the river
that carries us in its arms.
Tell me again why, at the edge
of the world, the wind screams.

CONTENTS

Dayenu 1

Carriers 71

Settlers 117

Allotments 157

Reconstruction 191

DAYENU

Dayenu. A song that's part of the Jewish
celebration of Passover:
"It would have been enough for us."

1.

At 10:36 as I'm listening to accounts on the radio of a plane lost over the Arctic Sea, the noise from within the trunk gets to be so annoying that I stop the car, open up and whack the guy with the cut-down baseball bat I stowed under the front seat. The ride's a lot better after that. They never find the plane.

Where I've pulled off is this little rise from which you can see the highway rolling on for miles in both directions, my very own wee grassy knoll. The trees off the road are at that half-and-half stage, leaves gone brown closer to the ground, those above stubbornly hanging on. Because of Union Day there's little traffic, two semis, a couple of vans and a pickup during the time I'm there, which is the only reason

I'm risking everything to be out here and on the road taking care of one last piece of business. Even the government's mostly on hold.

What they never understood, I'm thinking as I get back in the car, what it took me so long to understand, is that after rehab I became a different person. Not as in some idiotic this-changed-my-life blather, or that last two minutes of screen drama with light shining in the guy's eyes and throbs of music. *Everything* changed. How the sky looks in early morning, the taste of foods, longings you can't put a name to. Time itself, the way it comes and goes. Learning all over how to do the most basic things, walk, hold onto a glass, open doors, brush teeth, tie shoes, put your belt on from the right direction—all this reconfigures the world around you. A new person settles in. You introduce yourself to the new guy and start getting acquainted. It can take a while.

An hour later I make the delivery and go about my business, not that there is any. They'd got too close this time and I'd gone deeper to ground, pretty much as deep as one can burrow. The gig was a holdover from before, timing rendered it possible, so I took the chance. Messages left in various dropboxes now would grow up orphans.

I was staying on the raw inner edge of the city, a gaza strip where old parts of town hang on by their fingernails to the new, in a house with rooms the size of shipping crates. Tattoo-and-piercing parlor nearby, four boarded-up houses like ghosts of mine, an art gallery through whose windows you can see paintings heavy on huge red lips, portions of iridescent automobiles and imaginary animals.

Nostalgia, dreamland, history in a nutshell.

The house owner supposedly (this gleaned from old correspondence and visa applications) was away "hunting down his ancestry," driven by the belief that once he knows about his great-great-grandfather, his own blurry life will drift into focus. So here I am, with every item on the successful lurker's shopping list in place: semi-abandoned neighborhood, evidence of high turnover, no one on the streets, irregular or nonexistent patrols, no deliveries, few signs of curiosity idle or otherwise.

A week or so in, it occurred to me that the neighborhood had this fairy tale thing going. Grumpy old man half a block south, bighead ogre seen peering out windows of the house covered with vines, guy with cornrows who resided at the covered bus stop and could pass for a genie, even a little girl who lived down the lane.

Look at the same frame sideways, of course, and it goes immediately dark: poverty, political pandering, ineptitude, dispossession. Where you watch from, and how you look, dictates what you see.

A cascade of strokes, they told me. Infarctions.

Areas of tissue death brought on by interruptions in blood supply and oxygen deprivation—like half a dozen heart attacks moved far north. No problem, they said. We'll go in and fix this.

So they did.

THEY CAME FOR ME at 4 A.M. No traffic or other sounds outside; the curfews were in place. And nothing more than a promise of light in the sky. The third step of the second landing creaked. I made sure of that with a bit of creative carpentry when I moved in.

Four of them. I counted the creaks. Then was out the window and down, gone truly to ground, by the time the last one hit the landing.

We wait to be gathered, my uncle always said. Tribally, commercially, virtually, finally. Uncle Carl disappeared when I was eight, in one of the myriad foreign lands where we indulged what were then called police actions. Hard upon that, his footprints and afterimage began to leak away, public records, photographs, rosters. Within a matter of weeks he no longer existed.

Nothing in this old part of town had been planned. The alleyway in which I found myself was no exception; it simply came into being as buildings grew around it. Doorways, jury-rigged gates and doglegged side paths could lead nowhere. But exits abounded. I took one at random, looking back to where their cars (always two of them, it seemed, always dark gray) sat at curbside, still and featureless as skulls.

We wait to be gathered.

THAT DAY, DAYS BEFORE, the wind blew hard, tunneling down through the streets of the city bearing tides of refuse. Drink containers, bits of printout, feather and bone, scraps of clothing. Birds, mostly hawks, stayed put on building tops, electing not to launch themselves into the fray as, overhead, clouds collided and the large ate the small. I was on one of those building tops too, looking down at protestors who had gathered outside People's Hall, protestors largely in their late teens or early twenties, with a sampling from the next generation up sprinkled among them. Just over a hundred, I'd say, though news reports doubled that figure.

The police had military-issue equipment: weapons, body armor, full automatics, electrics. They waded into the kids, stunned a number of them, gassed the rest, now had them face down on the ground roughly in squares.

There are no right angles in nature.

We're never too far from the ground. My uncle again.

Watching events below so closely, I had failed to notice the drone hovering nearby, took note of it only when one of the hawks launched from a rooftop. The hawk hit hard. Its talons scrabbled for a hold but, finding no purchase, it flew on. Unable to right itself, the drone crashed into the side of a building. Though not before it had scanned me and dialed it in.

TULIPS.

In seventeenth century Holland, Uncle Carl told me, a single bulb of the rare *Semper Augustus* sold for the price of a good house. The tulip craze geared up in November 1636, ran its course, and burned itself out by February of the next year, forever a lesson on inflated markets, fabricated desire and greed of a sort not so much unlearned as endlessly learned and forgotten.

I was seven. This was a year or so before he was supposed to come back for a visit, for shore leave. Before he disappeared. Before he got gathered.

I had no idea what he was talking about, but I did have memories of earlier stories, stories that would adhere over time to experiences of my own, form a latticework upon which hung notions of life untempered by slogans, manipulation and misdirection.

I TOOK BREAKFAST AT a Quick'n'Easy, street name Queasy, directly across from the fast rail's inner loop, watching passengers flow onto the platform then drain into the maw of the cars or out onto the streets.

An abandoned building nearby, once a pharmacy, bore an arc of spray-painted letters on its front: REBORN. Another farther along, faded red and yellow colors suggesting it had once been a bodega, read

BELIEVE. Christians come into the neighborhood at night and leave their mark, evaporate like dew.

I'd barely settled in at a window seat on the 6:56 Express when the aisle seat beside me filled. We picked up speed; station, sky and buildings outside ran together in a single blurred banner. The light on the camera at the front of the car blinked steadily. I kept my face averted as though looking out the window. Not that this would help all that much, should they engage recognition software.

"Sorry to keep you waiting," I said without turning to my seat mate.

"Two hours, a smidge less. About as I expected. This was your most likely egress."

"You ran a sim?"

"No need. The dogs were closing in, I knew where, I had absolute confidence they'd fail. There was a time we thought alike."

"You might easily have called in the dogs yourself. Primed the pump."

"Ah, but that would lack subtlety. Not to mention it would leave my size ten footprints scattered about digitally. Still, there it was. And when was I likely ever to have another chance to find you?"

Security came through the car randomly checking, a young woman shiny with purpose, uniform pants pressed blade-sharp, and we stopped talking. Outwardly calm, within I was anything but. Flee if possible, fight if not. But she passed us by. Moments later the train slowed almost to a stop as we drew abreast of the war memorial. Passengers went about their business, chatting to companions, working or browsing on links. One woman's eyes never left the wall. She could not see the name, but she knew it was there. Husband? Sibling? Child? As the last row of names crawled by, the train regained speed. At the border between municipalities, guards waved us through.

We went down, temporarily, at West End Station. Sniffers had flagged probable contraband—illicit drugs or explosives, usually—so trains were held and passengers offloaded to the platform. We'd scarcely lined up behind the sensor gates when a young man near the end broke and ran, only to stop moments later as though he'd run into an invisible wall—the first time I'd seen the new electrics in action. Guards unsheathed a wafer-thin stretcher, rolled him bonelessly onto it and bore him away. Soon we were on the move again.

Warren waited till a teenaged Asian passenger, belt and backpack straps studded with what looked to be ancient revolver casings, passed.

"Here."

I took what he held out, a shape and weight familiar to my hand. Its cover creased and worn though it had to be new.

"A new name, history, vitals, the data manipulated just enough that scans won't flag it, but it's basically you. Most anywhere in the city and surround, these will suffice. You'll want to stay away from admin buildings, information centers." He turned to the window. "This would be your stop."

The announcement came then over the speakers. All our grand technology, and station calls still sound like hamsters gargling.

"Use the papers if you wish. If not, dispose of them. On the chance that you use them, Frances looks forward to seeing you."

I turned back and motioned for him to follow.

WE'RE SITTING IN A foxhole in some country with too many vowels in its name. Officially this is a TBH, Transport Battle Habitat, and doesn't have much of anything to do with foxholes, but that's what we call it. Made of some mystery plastic that goes hard when you inflate it and soft again when you go the other way. Full stealth optics: bends and reflects light to blend with the surround or disappear into it—woodland, plains, whatever. Desert's harder, of course, but you could almost feel the poor thing struggling, doing its best.

Fran is sniffing at an RP she just tore into. The pack itself looks like jerky or tree bark. A meaningless script of letters and numbers on it but no clue what waits inside. She tries to break off a piece of whatever it is and can't, pulls the knife out of her boot.

"Adventure," I say. "Suspense."

"Hey, chewing on this at least will give me something to do for half an hour." We hear the wheeze and hollow grunt of shells striking not too far off. "The boys are playing again."

"Ding dong the witch ain't dead."

"Just polishing her teeth."

"Shiny!"

Lots of time to talk out there. I know about her favorite toy when she was four or five, a plastic submarine with a compartment you filled with baking soda to make it dive and surface, dive and surface. The head made of a carved coconut with seashells for eyes and ears. Her first kiss—from a boy twice her age whose hand crawled roughly into her shorts. The twin brother who died in a bombing, in the coffee shop across the street from the college where he taught, when she was in boot camp.

"Everybody was going," she said when she told me about that. "My cat died. My brother. Our old man. Ever feel surrounded?"

I waited for a shell to hit, said "Nah" when one did.

Timing is everything.

She looks out the gun slot of the foxhole. "Dogs'll be next," she says.

The dogs were everywhere back then. Genetically manipulated, physical and mental augmentations. Ten or twelve of them would spill up over the horizon and surge toward you. Nothing short of heavy artillery stopped them. Even then, what was left of them, half dogs, forequarters, kept coming. Most of the time they couldn't see the foxholes but knew they were there—smelled them, sensed them.

These do what we hope: circle us twice, snuffle ground, sniff air, do it all again and move on.

"Damn things give me the willies every time," Fran says.

"They're supposed to. Bring you up against the elemental, the savage, within yourself."

"Deep waters, college boy. Good to see all that schooling wasn't wasted."

"Most of it was. But knowledge is like cobwebs, get close enough, some stick."

Our coms crackle. Go orders. Moments later we're over the top, on our way to finding the elemental and savage within ourselves.

AT NIGHT FORAGERS COME out, looking for food, cast-off clothing, machine parts, citizens marooned for whatever reason in their world—anything they can use. Theirs is a mission of salvage, scooping up leftovers, cast-offs, the discarded. They decline the housing, employment, health care and securities guaranteed to all, choosing to live invisibly, perilously, and when every few years the government extends offers of amnesty, those offers go ignored.

Walking away from the station into thinner ground and air, we passed a number of Foragers who looked on, even followed a bit, before concluding it unwise to approach.

Warren watched as one, a woman in her late teens or early twenties, face pale above an ankle-length dark overcoat, military issue, took a final look and withdrew. "Interesting lives," he said.

"They're a part of you, deep inside, that longs to scream *No*."

"Perhaps not so deep as you imagine." He touched a wall, ran his hand along it. Dark grit fell from the hand when he took it away. "How did we come to live in a world where everything is something else?"

"Other than what it seems? We've always lived there."

"Then how do choices get made?"

"Faith."

"Now there's something you can hold onto." He pulled out a link, looked for a moment at the screen, and replaced it. "Our plan to protect Frances—"

"By staging her death."

"—was solid, with high probability of success."

"Not that it would ever occur to others that it was a ploy."

He met my eyes, an action intended to register sincerity and directness but in effect defensive.

"*High probability* means you ran sims," I said, "as

many times as it took for someone to get onto those runs."

"Of course."

"Then you had the tag. Trawled out and put them down. It wasn't about protecting Fran."

We walked on. Pavement out here was everywhere cracked, fractured into multiple planes, grass and weeds growing from the fissures like trees on a hundred tiny hills.

"Afterward," Warren said, "she simply chose *not to*—much as you did."

Thinking I heard footsteps, I put out an arm to halt us. We stood quietly, breathing slowly. Nothing more came. "Do you know where she is?"

"No. Nor, we trust, do those attempting to kill her."

"You've intel?"

He shook his head. "Five words to a secure address. *Introduce me to your friend?*"

"A safe word."

"And her way of asking for you. A request she would make only . . ."

Around us, like his sentence, the city trailed off, neither quite there nor absent. Heaps of refuse that looked to be undisturbed. Little evidence of rats or other rodents—larger beasts who'd rarely venture closer to the city saw to that.

—

COLLEGE DAYS. STRAY BUNCHES of us had got our heads filled with notions of retrieving history, scrubbing away the years, getting back to common ground we'd misplaced. Music became a part of this; for about five minutes I played at being a musician. Fell in quickly with Sid Coleman, and while I wasn't ever much good and wasn't going to be, I could bite into a rhythm and never let go. We started out playing for parties, college gigs and such. Later, it was mostly protest meetings.

Sid steamed with frustration from the get-go. What he wanted to do was talk politics but what everyone else wanted was for him to bring his guitar and sing. He had started out with old-time mountain music, discovered calypso and Memphis jug bands, slid into home base with songs against what we started calling the forever wars. He sang right up to the day he got his notice. That day he put his guitar away for good.

Sid and his crew were chowing down on a breakfast of beer and RPs when mortar shells struck. Eight were killed. And while Sid escaped further injury, the blasts took his hearing. This was a couple of borders over from where we are now. It's all the same war, he used to sing, they just move it from place to place.

—Hang on, Fran said, I need to pee. She checked with the infrared scope for all clear and stepped out. Got back and said, Okay . . .

That's it. There isn't any more.

Oh.

But there was.

Years later, back home, I ran into Sid on the street. I could see in his face that he didn't remember me, though he claimed to. He wore fake fatigues, the kind they sell at discount stores, and bedroom slippers. His hair was carefully combed, with a sheen of oil that smelled rank. Don't get out much, he said. One social engagement on my calendar every month. On the fifteenth, 0900 to the minute, the government check lands in my account. No fanfare, no fail, there it is, egg plopped in the nest. And there I am too, waiting to claim my money.

SOMEONE HANDS YOU A gun, you don't check it out before you use it, be sure of its function, you're a fool. Same with false papers. Next morning I crossed the southeast border into Palms, a city with no industry or trade centers and of scant strategic interest, populated as it is by the aged afloat on their pensions.

Cities, like the civilizations they reflect, find their rhythm. Their surges, falls. Areas within falter, decline and bottom out, open to new strains of inhabitants and push their way back up. Palms for now was on hold, a single sustained note.

From town's center I walked out to the grand

artificial lake where picnic tables, benches and teeter-totters squatted at eight-meter intervals around clear water. Teeter-totters, one assumes, for visiting grandchildren, though that day there were none. Plenty of elderly folk at the tables or sitting with feet in the water on low-slung walls, people a generation or two younger standing by. Caretakers.

I ended up back in town at a sparsely populated outdoor café, server and barista of an age with those around. Bob, the server, put me in mind of old-time French waiters, professional mien and mantle donned with his apron. The barista's demeanor came from warmer climes; she tapped on cup bottoms, swiveled about, triggered the steamer in syncopated bursts as she worked. Mildred's a peach, Bob said, directing his gaze briefly that way when I commented.

A couple I'd estimate to be in their eighties sat across from one another at a table nearby, each with a link propped before. She'd key in something on hers, he'd look at his. They'd both look up and smile. Then it was his turn.

Children? Images from long ago—a vacation on the big island before the embargos, places they'd lived, concerts and celebrations attended, their younger selves?

Even stolid Bob registered their happiness, careful not to interrupt but repeatedly locating himself close by lest they need something.

A frail-seeming man in eyeglasses sat reading an actual book whose title I eventually made out to be *A History of Radical Thought*. Interesting, that use of the indefinite article, I thought, *a* instead of *the*; one had to wonder at the content. There could be so many such histories.

When Bob set down a tea cake at another table, the woman there waited for him to walk away then quickly bowed her head and, with one hand in half a moment, sketched a shape in the air before her chest: silent prayer, and what few would recognize as the sign of the cross.

Across the street, in a park bordered on the far side by offset stands of trees, two women in sundresses, a style I recalled from childhood, were flying a kite made to look like a huge frog and awash with bright yellows, crimson, metallic blues. The runner had just let go the kite; both laughed as the frog took to sky.

Smelling of fresh earth, rich and dark, the coffee was good. I had three cups, took another walk round the lake, and remounted the train without challenge or incident. On the trip back, mechanical or guidance problems delayed us, and it grew dark as we reached the city, lights coming on about us, curfew close enough to give concern. Officials waited on the platform to issue safe passes. Elsewhere, automatic weapons cradled in their arms, soldiers who looked to be barely out of adolescence patrolled.

2.

So there I am in a room, rooting about in the few personal belongings left behind, listening for footsteps outside in the hall or coming up stairs. How did I arrive here? We wonder that all our lives, don't we?

It was as much the idea of a room as it was a room. Plato and Socrates might have stood at the door arguing for days. A single small window set high, its plastic treated so that light blossomed as it passed through, flooded the room with virtual sunshine. From one wall a lower panel let down to become a bed, another panel above to serve as table or desk.

Where a man lives and what's inside his head, they're mirrors of one another, my trainers said. In which case there shouldn't be a whole lot going on in Merritt Li's. And if I had the right person, I knew *that* wasn't true.

My inventory disclosed a packet of expired papers and passes bound together in a drawer, a thin wallet containing recent travel visas, a drawerful of clothes, some disposable, some not, all of them dark and characterless. On his link I found itineraries and receipts, forty-six emails that seemed to be business related, though what business would be impossible to discern, and a young adult novel about the Nation Wars.

Elsewhere about the room, apportioned to the innards of various appliances, a Squeeze, a cooker, a coffee maker, I found what could only be the components of a stunner, cast in a hard plastic I'd not seen before, doubtless unkennable to scanners.

Immediately I became aware of a presence in the doorway behind me. There'd been no warning sounds, no footsteps. Right. So he had to be who and what I thought.

"We have mutual friends," I said, turning.

"Else you wouldn't be here."

Older than myself by a decade and more, conceivably old enough to remember the wars he'd been reading about. No sign of recognition at the safe word. Stance and carriage, legs apart, shoulders and hips in a line, confirmed other suspicions. Military.

I glanced up from his feet at the same time he did so from mine. Anticipating attack, one sees it begin there.

"Your belongings remain as they were," I said.

He nodded. Waited.

"Three days ago you were in Lower Cam, at a train stop where an attack took place. Two citizens were injured. The target, Frances diPalma, fled."

"Leaving a body behind her. That one not a bystander."

He held out both hands to signal non-aggression and, at my nod, stepped to the console to dial open the built-in screen. Habit—and of little benefit should we be on lens, but one takes the path available.

A spirited discussion of the city's economic status bloomed onscreen: female moderator, one man in a dark suit, one in a sky blue sweater. It's really quite simple, assuming you have the facts, the suit-wearer said. The other's expression suggested that not once in his life had he encountered anything other than complexity, nor could he anticipate ever doing so.

"You believe I was there to take her down," Merritt Li said.

"Yes."

"I was there, but to a different purpose than you suppose. She is in fact a mutual friend. I know her as Molly."

RUEFUL TUESDAY, TWO DAYS before. I had the windows dialed down while watching a feed on vanishing species. I sat back, dialed the window up, the screen down, to look across at the next building. Uncle Carl used to tell me a story about how this early jazz man, Buddy Bolden, threw a baby out the window in New Orleans and a neighbor leaned out his window and caught it. That's about how close we were.

For a moment I could make out moving shapes over there, people, before they dialed down *their* window.

I had punched back in for the sad tale of vanished sea otters and was remembering how when we'd first come here to the city, half-jokingly calling ourselves settlers, jumpy with wonder, with the effort and worry of fitting in, there'd been a linkstop showing disaster movies round the clock. World after world ravaged by giant insects, tiny insects, momentous storms, awakened deep-sea creatures, carnivorous plants, science, our own stupidity.

With no forewarning, otter, shore and sea contracted, siphoned down to a crawler.

Warren's face above.

"This," he said, then was gone.

Rosland, time stamp less than an hour ago. A train stop. Single tracks up- and downtown, a dozen people waiting. Strollers, shufflers. Solitary busker playing accordion, license pasted to his top hat, little movement otherwise. Then suddenly there was.

A man walked briskly toward a woman waiting by the uptown track. She turned, transformed at a breath from citizen to warrior, everything about her changing in that instant. She shifted legs and feet, leaned hard left as he fired, followed that lean into full motion.

Moments later, the man lay on the platform, face turned to the camera.

Then another face glancing back, gone as its owner sprinted up the walkway Fran had vanished into.

Merritt Li's face.

Whereupon Warren's returned.

"We think there were two other incidents, but this is the first we've had surveillance."

"Fran took one of the attackers down."

"Cleanly."

"The second attacker followed her."

"In the tunnel they're off lens. We lost them. Nothing topside, nothing on connected platforms."

"Any luck flagging her follower?"

"Check your drops. The bundle I sent should help with that."

"WE FOUGHT TOGETHER AT Kingston," Merritt Li said. "Deep penetration. She had the squad."

Doing what Rangers do.

"Not many walked away, either side." He thumbed the sound on the room's screen up a notch. "With the years, details have taken on a life of their own. You know the song?"

Two of them, actually. The official version, Kingston as a triumph of patriotism and the human spirit; the other underscoring the battle's death toll, social cost and ultimate pointlessness.

"Three of us came out of the fire. Two walking, one on Molly's shoulder."

Onscreen discussion of city economy had given way to the latest stats on immigration. Full-color graphs rolled across the screen. Authorities revoiced the stats and graphs: a marked uptick in Citizen Provisionals from rural regions far south, this fueled by border disputes among neighboring city-states. Graphics and voice-over were out of synch. Technician error, I thought. Then for a moment before getting shut down, voice and content changed drastically. Revisionist overdubs. Official news reestablished itself.

Li pointed to the screen, one of the southern borders. Drones from a couple generations back floated above scattered groups of ragged troops and rioters.

"I'm supposed to be there. Just about now, my CO is discovering I'm not."

Even those you never see cast shadows. What I'd had were forests of filters and firewalls, limited access to public records and no idea at all to whom his allegiance belonged, or if he might be off the grid entirely. But I also had Li's face, by extrapolation his body volumes, and the way his body moved. It had taken me the best part of the two days since Warren dialed in with the clips, and a sum of chancy data diving, to find him.

"I assume your story varies little from my own," Li said.

"Little enough."

He waited a moment, then went on.

"One of my links stays on free scan, reach-and-grab for anything that hints of undisclosed military activity. Tagged one that felt half solid. Then another came through ringing like bells. Not much to doubt there. A takedown, and good—but it didn't work. And seeing how it unrolled, I knew why. Molly. That first time too, I figured, so now they'd come at her twice and she put them down. They'd be getting ready to kick it into overdrive."

"You have any idea why she was targeted?"

"It's not like we were sending Union Day cards to one another, with a nice write-up about our year."

"Right. Time to time, I'd hear things. She married and had a family up in Minnesota or Vancouver. She was consulting for or riding herd on private companies. She'd taken up teaching. Until last week, as far as I knew, she was dead."

"While on assignment."

"What we all heard. Turns out we weren't the only ones."

Li didn't react, didn't ask where that came from.

The pieces were falling together in his mind. "A crawler," he said.

"Followed by full-frontal assault. Once that closed down, Fran elected to stay off chart."

"The moves on her could be flashback from that."

"Could be."

"And we don't know who the crawler found."

"What we know between us doesn't take up much space in the world."

Li glanced back at the screen. Forsaken drones. Ragtag troops and rioters. "Everything's like paper folded so many times you can't tell what it is anymore."

I remembered Warren's rhetorical *How did we come to live in a world where everything is something else?*

"Molly called out to you," Li said.

"Relayed a message with a trigger word." I told him much of the rest as well.

"Wanted you at her back."

"As you said, they'll be stepping it up."

"And you came to me."

Yes.

"So now she has us both."

"Or will have."

Li pulled his duffel from a shelf by the door. "Not much here I can't leave behind. Give me ten minutes. Molly, you, me. Damn near have the makings of a volunteer army here, don't we? A militia—just like that hoary old piece of 1787 paper said."

3.

What I remember is questions, questions that should have been easy enough but weren't, and I had no idea why. What is today's date? Do you know where you are? It took time before I realized the voices were speaking to me. They were voices beamed in from some far-off world that had nothing to do with me, grotesque half-faces hovering over me, random collections of features that changed and changed again.

Do you know where you are?

No—but at some point I began looking about for clues. Hospital, I said early on, but that wasn't good enough.

Gradually I came to understand that at the end of each night shift someone wrote the new day's date on a whiteboard at one side of the room along with the physician, RN and NA assigned that shift, so pretty soon (with no idea what *soon* in this circumstance might encompass) I had that much covered.

Progress.

Good boy.

They were *so* pleased.

Over time, too, I learned to fake recognition of staff members, and to look for the hospital's name, which I never could keep hold of in my mind, on nametags.

Yep, I know where I am all right.

And it's the twenty-first. (Though if they pushed for day of the week I foundered. That wasn't on the whiteboard.)

Seizures? I answered. Stroke?

Then the questions got harder. After which they said let's go for a walk why don't we, an absurd goal given my inability to turn unassisted in bed or move my legs, the physical therapist's verbal commands meeting with no greater success in converting directive to action than those coursing along my nervous system.

This page currently unavailable.

Please try again later.

Error.

But I needed ambulation to qualify for further rehab. So therapist Abraham sandbagged me into sitting position, hauled me to our feet and, with mine dragging and scraping at the floor, carried me the required half dozen steps, the unlikeliest dance partners ever.

We were on our fifth, maybe sixth provisional government by then. Some were ill-advised, rapidly imploding coalitions, so . . . five, six, seven, who can be sure? This one had begun to look as though it might stick, like the stray cat that follows you home and, once fed, stays.

I learned that later, of course.

Three worlds, Abraham said, coexist. There was the old world of things as they are—of acceptance, of discipline, where we take what pleasure exists in what we have and expect no more. There was the new world, in which everything, country, selves, the world's very face, becomes endlessly reinvented, remade, refurbished. And now this third world struggling to be born, where old world and new will learn to live with one another.

Like Abraham and myself scuttling across the hospital's tiled floors.

I'm not supposed to be talking like this, Abraham said.

We were on a break, and he'd pushed me outside, to a patio bordered by scrubby bushes and smelling of rosemary, where with minimal help I'd successfully tottered from the wheelchair and stumbled five terrifying steps to a bench. Applause would have been in order.

I asked if reinventing myself was not what I was doing.

More like rebuilding, he said. Refurbishing.

When I was a child, living in the first of our many homes, money was aflow, families and the neighborhood on their way up. If you tore a house down entire, you had to apply for new building permits. Leave one wall standing, it could pass as a remodel. So crews arrived in trucks and on foot to swarm over the site, piles of roofing, earth, brick and siding appeared, and within days, where the Jacobs or Shah house had been, there stood, in moonlight among hills of rubble, the ruins of a single wall.

Ready to get back to work? Abraham said. Patiently they await: leg lifts, stationary cycling, weights, countless manifestations of pulleys and resistance. Row . . . Pull . . . Hold . . . Hold. Stepping over minefields of what look like tiny traffic cones. Balancing atop a footboard mounted on half a steel ball. Both of those last while clinging to walk bars and waiting for the state to wither away as Abraham said the old books predicted.

But five weeks further in, buckets of sweat lost to history, I've still not progressed past totter, trip and hope like hell I'll make it to the bench. A convocation gets called. The physician I've taken to thinking of as Doc Salvage is spokesperson. Real name's something with too many *s*'s or *z*'s or both, but to me he's Doc Salvage. Here's the story, he begins. He smiles, then puts away the smile so it won't get in the way of what he has to say.

They fully appreciate the work I've done. My attitude. My doggedness. My determination. They know I've hung on like a snapping turtle and refused to let go. The consensus is that we (pronoun modulating now to first-person plural) have gone as far as might reasonably be expected. In short, I can stay as I was, with severely diminished capacities, or.

Or being that I undergo an experimental procedure.

They would reboot and reconnect synapses, restore neural pathways, rewire connections that had failed to regenerate autonomously. And while they were in there they'd go ahead and rearrange the furniture. Spruce things up here and there. New carpet, fresh paint.

You have the technology to do that? I asked.

We do.

And I'll be myself again, physically?

A better version. Though we understand (the smile is back) that sentimentally you may be attached to the present one.

And what of risks? Complications?

Oh, nothing terribly untoward. More or less the

standard OR checklist: bleeds, infection, drug reactions. A long recovery.

You've all this certainty, with an experimental procedure?

Life itself is an experimental procedure. As you know.

And I've already had a long recovery.

Ah, that. Fundamentally you will have to start over, I'm afraid. Begin again.

And so I did in subsequent months as Doc Salvage and crew watched closely to assess development and as I pushed harder at my limits than I'd ever have thought possible. We were down in the swirly deep, in the sludge, as Abraham deemed. But within weeks the leg that before could scarcely clear the floor now could kick higher than my head, I could hop across the room, steady as a fence post, on a single foot, and fingers could pick bits of straw from off the tabletop. I could climb, crawl, swim, run, lift.

And wonder at what I'd been told, what I'd not.

You've taken note, Doc Salvage said six months later, how little resistance there is for you in physical activity.

Uncharacteristically, window shades were up behind him and light streamed in, so that he appeared to have a halo about his body, or to be going subtly out of focus.

All much as we anticipated, he said. But it is far from being the story's end.

He paused, letting the moment stretch. Something reflective passed outside, a car, a copter, a drone, tossing stabs of light against the rear wall.

Our bodies teem with censors built and inculcated into us, Doc Salvage continued, censors that create distraction, indecision, delay—drag, if you will. Morality. Cultural mores. Emotions. Most particularly the last. And we have learned how to bypass those. Eliminate the drag. We can peel away emotions, mute them, dial them down to the very threshold.

As, he said, we've done with you.

Which explained a lot of what had been going on in body and mind, things I'd been unable to put into words.

I now fit, they believed, a container they'd made for me.

But already, even then, I was spilling from it.

THEY HAD GIVEN ME something. They had taken something. On such barter is a society founded. How much control over our lives do we retain, how much cede to the state? What debts do we take on in exchange for the state's benefits? How does the state balance its responsibilities to the individual and to the collective? To what degree does it exist to serve, to what degree to oversee, its citizenry?

Theories grinding against one another in the dark.

The truth is this: Our enemies at the time were

messing about with neurotoxins. It was those neurotoxins, not a CVA, not seizures as I'd been told, that came upon me in the burned-out fields of the far northwest. Those upon whose reach I was borne to the government hospital to awaken empty, blank and helpless, isolate fragments of the world cascading around me.

The truth is this as well: I was changed. By the gas. By Doc's procedure. By the experience of reinhabiting my own body. And later, by my actions.

Only with time did I come to understand the scope and nature of the changes within. Doc was right that emotions no longer obscured my actions; about much else he was wrong.

A single image remains from before medics scooped me up. I am dragging myself across stubble. I can hear nothing, feel nothing. My legs refuse to function. And all I can see—this fills my vision—are my arms out before me. They stretch and stretch again. Each time I pull my body forward, they stretch more. My hand, my fingers, are yards away, meters, miles. And I do not advance.

But within a year of that meeting with Doc Salvage I was on the move. There was much, in this fledgling nation, to be done.

THE LAMENTATIONS OF OLD men forever fall deaf on youngster's ears, my uncle said. He knew that early.

Sometimes I imagine myself an old man tied by sheets into my chair in the dayroom of a care center speaking—even though there is no one listening, no one there to listen—about the things I did, things I refused to do, things I never quite recovered from doing.

At a table nearby, two men and a woman play cards, some game in which single cards get dealt back onto the table. In at least ten minutes no one's put down a card. It's the woman's turn. The men sit unmoving, hands before them, cards fanned. They could be mannikins propped there. On the screen across the dayroom a giant face says she loves us, in the same movie that plays at this time every Tuesday, but no one cares.

How does one assay right and wrong? With change crashing down all around us, do the words even have meaning?

Is everything finally relative?

What would you give, Sid Coleman used to sing, *in exchange for your soul?* An old, old song.

I know that the world of which I speak sitting here tied into my chair would be unrecognizable to the young. Unrecognizable to most anyone, really, should they chance to be around to hear. And as I speak, I watch cockroaches scuttling on the wall, lose my thoughts, begin to wonder about the cockroach's world. They've been around forever, never changed.

All this, of course, knowing that I will never be an old man.

4.

"This is your place?"

"Borrowed. Property is theft—right?"

Out on the farthest edge of the city. Forager territory. Dog-pack-and-worse territory. I looked about at the cot, racks of storage cells, plastic units stacked variously to form furniture of a sort. All of it graceless and functional, the sole concession to domestication being a plaque hung on a side wall and jiggered to look like an old-time sampler: *Always Drink Upstream of the Herd.*

"You can't be here often, or for extended periods. What happens when you're not?"

"I have guard rats." He began pulling cubes from one of the stacks. "Joking. About theft and property, too." He reconfigured the cubes as a chair, more or less. "Those who live out here and I have an understanding. Turns out we've much in common."

"Being?"

"That you deal with an unfree world by making yourself so free that your very existence is an act of rebellion. Camus, I think."

"Yet you run with the marshals of that world."

"Their screens, drones and watchers catch most of what happens on the surface of their world. But much goes on beneath, in ours."

"Giants of the deep?"

"Minnows and small fish. Thousands upon thousands of us. Where the true history resides."

Li pulled a link from his pocket, punched in.

"The villagers want to climb the hill and storm the castle, and there is no castle. The castle is all around us. What we have to do is learn to live in it."

As he spoke, perfectly relaxed, he was sweeping and scanning at impressive speed. "Ever come across a series of children's books, *Billy's Adventures*?"

I shook my head.

"I read them when I was five, six. The first one started off: 'Two years it was that I lived among the goats. Two years that I went about on all fours, ate whatever came before me.' Like most kid's books, as much as anything else they were put out there as socializers. Teach the boys and girls how to get along with others, shore up received wisdom, hip-hurrah things-as-they-are. But scratch the surface and what was underneath gave the lie to what was on top. The books weren't about joining the march, they were about staying apart while appearing to fit in. They were profoundly subversive."

Back when this area was a functioning part of the city, Li's squat had been a service facility, a utilities satellite maybe, a goods depot. Layers of steel shelving six and eight units deep sat against the rear wall. Stained and worn cement floors, splayed heads of ancient cables jutting from the wall. Steel everywhere, of a grade not seen for better than half a century, including the door that now rang open to admit an elderly man in clothing at once suggestive of tie-dye and camouflage. Balding, I saw as he slipped off his cloth cap.

"And so here you are back with us," the man said. Trace of a far-northern accent in his voice. "And not alone."

Li introduced us. "Thank you for minding the burrow, Daniel—as ever."

"Well then, we can't have just anyone moving in here, can we? We do have standards." Then to me: "Welcome to the junkyard."

Li had continued to monitor his link as we spoke. Now he beckoned me. The screen showed a street in the central city, masses of people moving along, dodges, feints, near-collisions.

"There," Li said. The cursor became an arrow, touched on one individual moving at a good clip close to storefronts and walls. "And there." Two larger figures, perhaps six meters back, matching speed with the first. "I'm piggybacked on security feeds. Seconds ago, sniffers at the corner dinged."

"Those two are armed."

We watched as the lone figure turned into a narrow side street or entryway. Both pursuers hesitated at the mouth, then stepped in, first one, then, on a six count, the other. People streamed by on the sidewalk. We waited. Moving at an easy pace, the single, smaller figure emerged. Patently she'd taken note where the cameras were and kept her face averted, but size and carriage were unmistakable.

Fran.

Molly.

"By now she's in the wind and the area's spilling over with police."

"And those hunting her will have new dogs in the area along with them," Li said. "Unless, of course, they're the same." He thumbed over to news feeds. No mention of the incident. Then to the city's official feeds, where delays from technical problems had been reported in the area and citizens were advised to consider alternate routes. "So many multiple realities," Li said. "Is it any wonder we're unable to see the world straight on?"

TIME PASSED, AS IT will, however hard one holds on.

Li told me about religious practices among the Melanese who, during old wars and due to the island's tactical location, grew accustomed to airplanes arriving almost daily filled with goods, some of which got shared, much of which got cast off and reclaimed. For many years after, with that war over, the islanders carved long clearings like runways in the forest, built small fires along them to either side, constructed a wooden hut for a man to sit in with wooden disks on his ears as headphones and bamboo shoots jutting out like antennae. They waited for the airplanes to return with goods. Everything was in place. Everything was just as before. But no airplanes came.

It began to feel as though what we were doing in our approach to the whole Fran-Molly affair wasn't far removed.

Why would Fran signal for backup then fail to make contact, even to make herself visible? Leapfrog, maybe? Assuming we'd move in and her pursuers' focus would shift to us, leaving her free to . . . what?

Look again.

There had been urgency, power, in that attack. The air crackled with it. Fran knew where cameras were placed, carefully kept her face averted. From visual evidence her pursuers also knew, yet took little effort to skirt the cameras. (1) They were protected or (2) They didn't exist.

And just what did we hope to learn by endlessly reviewing the incident? "One works with what one has," Li said every time we thumbed up the file.

What we had was next to nothing.

And hellhounds on our trails. We could all but hear them snuffling around out there in the dark.

5.

Government after government fell, each trailing in its wake the exhausted spume of grand theories. Anomie had come piecemeal over so long a time that we were hard-pressed to remember or imagine another way. Platitudes, slogans and homilies had supplanted thought. That, or unfocused, unbridled hatred.

Was the government at which we arrived a better one, or were we simply too exhausted to go on? The bigfish capitalism we fled and the overseer government we embraced had much the same disregard for bedrock democratic principles. But each individual was housed, educated to the extent he or she elected, provided sustenance and medical care, state-sponsored burial.

Border disputes, blockades, financial sloughs, outright attacks, the collapse of alliances. Those early years thrummed with dangers to which our nascent union, fussily jamming the day, often reacted with little regard for long-term consequence.

Ever on the go, the world's contours shifting and reshaping themselves even as I passed among them, I grew accustomed to media and official reports of a world far removed from that I witnessed. Which among these gaping disparities were sinister, which utilitarian? And just what was it I was doing out there? The people's work? The government's? That of a handful of wizards behind the curtain? One of Sid Coleman's songs comes to mind again, "Which Side Are You On," not all that much of a song really, but a damned good question. I wonder every day.

I was a good soldier, as soldiers go. One would expect years of such service to fix in place conventional, conservative beliefs. Instead, they honed within me an innate aversion to authority and to organizations in general. When I rummage in the attics of my mind, what I come up with is an immiscible regard for personal and civil liberty.

CLAETON, PRONOUNCED CLAYTOWN BY locals, mid-January and so cold that when your nose dripped, icicles formed. A thick white mist rose permanently from the ground. Bare trees loomed in the distance, looking as though someone had strung together a display of the hairless legs and knobby knees of old men. We inhabited a ghostly sea bottom.

Hansard and I were squirreled down in a scatter of boulders where a mountain range ran out into flatlands. There was one pass through the range and a patrol from Revisionist forces was on it. We were waiting for them.

Everyone knew the satellites were up there, circling tirelessly, bloated with information. And if satellites monitored even this afterbirth of a landscape, I told Hansard, they had to be watching us as well—not us here, us everywhere. Hansard shrugged and squeezed a nutrient pack to start it warming.

Drones might have dealt with the patrol, of course. Quickly. Efficiently. But drones hadn't the dramatic effect of a couple of warriors suddenly appearing at the mouth of the cave. Something in our blood and ancestral memory—others of our kind come for us.

Hansard finished drinking his nutrient, rolled the pack into a compact ball and stuffed it in a cargo pocket. The wind rose then, mist swirling like huge capes, cold biting into bones. Go codes buzzed in the bones behind our ears.

WE COULDN'T PRONOUNCE THE name of the place but were told it translated as Daredevil or Devil-May-Care. Biting cold had turned stewpot hot, barren landscape to cramped and crowded city. The stench of used-up air was everywhere. You could smell bodies and what they left behind. Sweat mixed with fine grit, pollen and laden gases and never went away. It coated your body, a hard film, a second skin that cracked when you moved. Hansard, rumors said, had gone down up here near the Canadian border some weeks before.

That time, we almost failed to make it out, beating a retreat through disruptions turning ever more chaotic (dodging raindrops, an old Marxist might have said) hours before the region tore itself apart, this being what happens when a government eloquently tottering on two legs gets one of them kicked out from under.

THEY CAME FOR US on the bullet train in Oregon. I turned from the window where sunlight shone blindingly on water, blinked, and there they were. Boots, jeans, Union jackets with the patches torn off. I've a brief memory of Tomas aloft, zigzagging toward the car's rear on the backs of the seats, right foot, left, starboard, port, before I turned to confront the others. All became in that instant clear and distinct. I could see the tiniest bunching of a muscle in the shoulder of one before that arm moved, see another's eyes tip to the left before head and body followed, sense the one about to bound directly toward me from all but imperceptible shifts in footing and posture.

I remember condensation on windows from the chill inside the car, the wide staring eyes of a child.

Afterward, we liberated a pickup from a parking lot nearby and rode that pale horse into Keizer to be about our business.

YEARS AFTER THAT DAY in Oregon, and as many more after what I'm recounting here, Fran and I stand where Merritt Li died. In those years, wildness has reclaimed that edge of the city. Sunlight spins toward us off the lake to our left as though in wafer-thin sheets. Spanish moss beards the branches of water oaks populated by dove and by dun-colored pigeons that were once city birds. Fran touches another oak near us; scaly ridges of its bark break off in her hand.

We're the only ones, she says.

Who will remember, I say.

It's become rote now.

No memorials for such as Merritt Li.

Only memory.

For another who has been erased. Who has been gathered. And for a time before Fran speaks again, we are quiet. Our voices drift away into the call of birds, the sough of wind.

Our kind were redundant before and will be again.

As the successful revolutionary must always be, right?

Okay. She laughs. *They can be redundant too.*

A heron floats in over the trees and lands at water's edge. A heron! Who would have believed there were herons left? I see the same light in Fran's eyes as in mine. Still, after all that has happened in our lives, we have the capacity for surprise, for wonder.

6.

When I was eleven, a contrarian even then, I made a list of all the stuff I never wanted to see again on TV and in movies. Wrote it out on a sheet of ruled paper, signed and dated the document and submitted it to my parents.

People jumping just ahead of flames as house, car, pier, ship or what-have-you explodes.

The disarming of bombs with everyone else sent away as our hero or heroine sweatily decides which wire to cut.

Police or soldiers putting down their guns in hostage situations.

Hostage situations.

The cop, finally pushed to his/her limit, tossing badge or detective's shield onto his/her CO's desk.

The cast, be they doctors, lawyers or cops, all striding side by side, often in slow motion, along a corridor on their way to another fine yet difficult day as credits roll.

"I wanted to give back."

"This is your chance to do the right thing."

"You're not going to die on me!"

How with two minutes left in the show the bad guy tells us why he's done all he has, that it's all justified.

The original screed ran two pages. In following years, amendments—additions, truthfully—added another fourteen, growing ever more prolix until attentions strayed elsewhere. From time to time as I submitted new editions, I requested progress reports from my parents. Could he have been so innocent, that fledgling contrarian, as to believe some channel existed whereby they might actually deal with these issues? Was he attempting to bend the world to some latent image he had in mind? Just to shout out to the world: *I am here*? Whatever else it may have presaged, the project attests that at least, even then, I was paying attention.

By this time I'd got heavily into reading and may have had at the back of my mind, like that movement in the room's corner you can't locate when looking straight on, intimations of how powerfully words affect—how they give form to—the world about us.

I became aware that my greatest pleasure lay not in what was happening within the confines of the narrative but in its textures: the surround, the moods and rhythms, the shifting colors. And that it was auxiliary characters I found most interesting. A quiet rejection of celebrity, maybe—this sense that those spun out to screen's edge, the postmen, foils, second bananas, loyal companions and walk-ons, are the ones who matter? History with its drums and wagons and wars marches past, and we go on scrabbling to stay in place, huddled with our families and tribes, setting tables, trying to find enough to eat.

Sheer plod makes plow down sillion shine, Gerard Manley Hopkins wrote. Not that, when you come down to it, we do a hell of a lot of shining. At best we give off just enough light to hold away the dark for an hour or two. That's all the fire Prometheus had to give us.

LIGHT WAS FAILING, IF never the fire, as Merritt Li and I made our way on glistening streets, cleaving insofar as we could to shadow and walls. Rain had begun hours earlier. Streetlights shimmered with halos, windows wore jackets of glaze—as would lens. That gave small comfort at the same time that the fact of fewer bodies abroad gave caution.

We weren't following leads so much as what someone once called wandering to find direction and someone else called searching for a black hat in a pitch-black room.

Rain made a rich stew of a hundred smells. Took away edges and corners and the hard surface of things. The city was feeling its way toward beauty.

There did seem to be a rudimentary pattern, the attacks moving outward from city's center, but patterns, what's there, what's not, can't be trusted. Apophenia. The perception of order in random data. See three dots on an otherwise blank page, right away you're trying to fit them together. Nonetheless, we were trolling in rude circles toward the outer banks, touching down at rail stations, pedestrian nodes, crossroads and terminals of every sort. That amounted to a lot of being out there in the open, exposed, and as chancy for Li as for me at this point, but (returning to a prior observation) what else did we have?

In such situations, while outwardly you're alert to every small shift or turn, changes in light, in movements around you, your own heartbeat or breathing, inwardly you're floating free, allowing your mind to do what it does best unpinned. Thoughts skitter, burn and flare out, some shapeless, others barbed. As I scurried from sillion to sillion, bench to stairway to arcade, thoughts of childhood, books, folk songs, populism and political exhaustion accompanied me.

All I wanted was for my life, when you picked it up

in your hands, to have some weight to it, Fran once told me. Rain coming down then outside our TBH as it was now on city streets, the two of us waiting for nightfall and go codes, foxhole reeking of processed food, stale air, unwashed bodies.

Within months of that, the GK virus had carved away fully a sixth of our population, especially among the elderly, infants and the chronically ill, all those with compromised immune systems, poor general health, low physical reserves.

Explanations for the virus? Natural selection at work in an overpopulated world, willful thinning of the herd by intellectual or financial elitists, Biblical cleansing, our own current government's research gone amiss, biologic agents introduced by any of a dozen or more current enemies.

Or that old friend happenstance.

Substantive as they were, Li's and my excursions had yielded little more than an anecdotal accounting of the city as it stood, along with instances of kindness, cruelty, anxiety and insouciance in fairly equal measure, in every conceivable shape or form.

Crews were busily tearing out the forest of digital billboards at city center, these having recently been judged (depending on the assessor) unaesthetic or ineffective.

The dry riverbed, cemented over years ago, was now being uncemented on its way to becoming a canal complete with boats and waterside city parks. Government-stamped posters with artists' renditions of the final result hung everywhere. Those of a cynical disposition well might wonder where funds for this massive project originated. More positive souls might choose not to take note of the disrepair in surrounding streets.

Repeatedly as we moved through the city we encountered flash-mob protests. Participants assembled without preamble at rail stations, on street corners, in the city's open spaces. Most protestors were young, some looked as though they'd awakened earlier in the day from Rip Van Winkle naps. They'd demonstrate, sometimes with silence and dialogue cards, other times with chants or improvised songs, and within minutes fade back into the crowd, before authorities showed up.

"We're chasing shadows at midnight," Merritt Li says one day.

And I hear Fran, another day, another time, saying "We're the shadow of shadows."

We'd come in country under cover of night, the two of us, and trekked on foot miles inland. The sky was starting to lighten and birds to sing when we reached the extraction point. Joon Kaas had not spoken a word the whole time, from the moment we breached his room. He had looked up and nodded, risen and gone ahead of us when signaled to do so.

Now at the clearing he lowered his head, to pray I think, before meeting Fran's eyes (instinctively aware she was prime) and nodding again, whether in surrender or some fashion of absolution I can't say.

"He knew," she said after.

That we were coming. Of course he did. And how it had to end.

Later I would understand that for most of his countrymen, thousands of them cast onto the streets and huddled together in houses, the eternally poor and forgotten, those without influence who went on scratching out a bare subsistence as terrible engines fell to earth all around them, Joon Kaas was a savior. With his passing, much of what he had worked to put in place, his challenges to privilege and to authority, new laws and mandates, new protections, began one by one to disappear.

PERHAPS MORE THAN ANYTHING else, we've enslaved ourselves to the grand notion of progress. In our minds we've left behind yesterday's errors, last year's lack of knowledge and crude half measures. Now we're headed straight up the slope, getting better and better, getting it right. But really we go on hauling along these sacks of goods we can't let go of, can't get rid of, tearing apart our world only to rebuild it to the old image.

In 1656 Spinoza was excommunicated from

Amsterdam's Portuguese-Jewish congregation for inveighing against those who promoted ignorance and irrational beliefs in order to lead citizens to act against their own best interests, to embrace conformism and orthodoxy, to surrender freedom for security. This, even though Dutch society had long agreed upon liberty, individual rights and freedom of thought. Four hundred years down the road, not much has changed. Same hazard signs at the roadside. Same crooked roads.

IT WAS IN THE last months of the struggle, while I was over the border in Free Alaska commandeering armaments, that I first felt the gears slipping. Four degrees coldly Fahrenheit outside. With a wind that felt to be removing skin slice by micrometric slice. Fortunately I was inside, and alone, when it happened, having just entered a safe house there. I remembered walking in and stepping toward the bathroom. Now I was on the floor, with urine puddled about me. How long? Five, six minutes by my timer. Vision blurred—a consequence of the fall? Taste of metal, copper, in the back of my throat. And I couldn't move.

That was far too familiar, a replay of week after week in rehab, frantically sending messages to legs, arms and hands that refused to comply, Abraham urging me on.

I doubt the immobility lasted more than a minute, but hours of panic got packed into it. I began to remember other stutters and misfires, each gone unremarked at the time. Now they took on weight, bore down.

"What are you thinking?" Fran will ask not long after, on our visit to Merritt Li's final foothold.

"An old sea diver's creed," I tell her, unsure myself of the connection, thinking of the fighters we took down there, of Merritt Li going down, of my own fall and my jacked-up system, "the one thing a diver forgets at great peril: If it moves, it wants to kill you."

Then I tell her what happened at the safe house, what it means. Simple physics, really. Put more current in the wire, it burns out faster.

"When did you know?"

"From the first, at some level—wordlessly. One sleepless morning in Toledo I got up, tapped in and pulled the records. I wasn't supposed to be able to do that. They had little idea what I could do."

I, the soft machinery that was me, was failing. Sparks failed to catch, messages misfired, data was corrupted.

I had, I supposed, a few months left.

7.

We never knew how Merritt Li came to be there.

His and my courses were set so as to bring the two of us together, close enough to rendezvous anyway, every three hours. When he didn't show at the old waterworks, I went looking. We both carried ancient low-frequency 'sponders we thought wouldn't be tapped. Guess we were wrong. They knew I was coming.

He had two of them back against a wall of stacked, partly crushed vehicles, tanklike cruisers from the last century. Two others, halfway across a bare dirt clearing hard as steel, had turned away to intercept me. Where numbers five and six came from I have no idea, they dropped out of nowhere like Dorothy.

A couple of them had weapons we'd never seen, the kind that, if you go looking, don't exist. Focused toxin's my guess. Or some fry-brain electronic equivalent. I saw nothing, no muzzle flash, no recoil, no exhaust, when one of those locked on Li lifted his handgun, but I saw the result. Li went down convulsing, limbs thrashing independently as though they belonged to different bodies.

Three of the four coming for me fell almost at the same time, one down, two down, three, without sound or obvious reason. Once I'd dealt with the fourth and looked again, the two by Li were on the ground and still. The whole sequence in just under sixteen seconds.

Movement atop a battered steel shed to the right took my attention, as it was meant to do.

Never show yourself against the sky.

Unless you're purposefully announcing yourself, of course.

She came down in three stages, over the side and catch with the left, swing to the right, drop and turn. Faultless as ever. No sign of what weapon she'd used. I recalled her late interest in antiquities, blowpipes and the like. One violinist wants shiny new and perfectly functional, another's always looking for old and funky, an instrument that makes you work to get the music out.

Her hair was cropped short and had tight curls

of gray like steel filings in it. The row of geometrical earrings, circle, square, triangle, cross, was gone from the left ear. Otherwise not much had changed. Musculature stood out in the glisten of sweat on her skin. Yellow T-shirt, green pants.

"Interesting choice of clothing for someone doing her best to be invisible."

"Figured if it came to it and I stood dead still, they might take me for a vegetable."

Blood had pooled in Li's face, turning it purple, then burst in a scatter of darker splotches across it. Limbs were rigid. No respiration, no pulse. A pandemic of that: No pulse or respiration in the ones she'd put down either.

"Here we go leaving a mess behind us," I said.

"Ah, well."

"With a bigger mess waiting ahead."

"Ah, well again." She snatched the mystery weapons from those by Li. "We hit the floor with whoever shows up on our dance card." Then looked around. "No eyes out here. No trackers."

"Chosen for it. So they're not government."

"Who can say?" At the time we believed them to be a single team, didn't understand there were three factions at work, a tangle of forces.

Fran had dropped to a squat and was breaking down one of the weapons. "Indications are, they think of themselves as freedom fighters. Then again, who doesn't? Freedom from taxes, bureaucracy, using the wrong texts at school? Or maybe they just want to tear the house down. Maybe we should have asked them."

She stood and brought over the gutted weapon. "Ever seen a power source like that?" A bright blue marble with no apparent harness or connection, spinning gyroscopically in a chamber not much larger than itself. "Have to wonder what else they have."

"Six less footmen, for a start."

"There'll be backup. We should be missing."

"Missing, we're good at."

"Have been till now."

She retrieved the second weapon and we started away. Darkness had begun unfurling from the ground and the air smelled of rain. Insects called to one another from trees and high grass, invisibly.

"When I was a child," Fran said, "no more than four or five, there was a cricket that sang outside my window every night. I'd go to bed, lie there in the dark and listen to it sing, night after night. Then one night it didn't. I knew it was dead, whatever dead was, and I cried."

Fran as a child, crying, I could scarcely picture. "Why were these six, and the others, on you?"

She pulled the power source from the first weapon, discarded its carcass. "They weren't."

She'd been working a private job much like that

of mine back before the team in dark gray cars came for me, and stumbled onto something that wasn't right. She finished the job and took to side roads, kicking over traces till she realized that both job and not-rightness were come-ons. Hand-tied lures, she said, designed to bring her out. So out she came. They were stalking her. She was stalking them, coming in and out of sight. Getting a fix on them. Who they might be, how many.

"They were moving around in teams, randomly, and about where you'd expect, train stations, transfer points. They'd see me, hang back, never close. Which was how I knew it went deeper. So I stepped it up."

"And they stepped in."

"Maybe they got impatient. Maybe like me they decided to push to see what pushed back. And I sent a message up the line to you—which is what they anticipated."

By this time we were moving toward the central city but on back streets long forsaken, block after block of abandoned warehouses and storage facilities from a past in which people were driven to accumulate so much that it spilled over. We'd spotted a few stragglers of the kind that, once seen, quickly vanish. Tree dwellers brought to earth, I think of them, on the ground but never quite of this world.

8.

A razor-cold January morning. Snow falling past the windows—silently, but you can't help looking that way again and again, listening. How could something take over the world to such degree and make no sound? The room's warmth moved in slow tides toward the windows, tugging at our skin as it passed by. Even the machines were silent as I did my best to become one with them.

Abraham watched and paced me, speaking in low tones about Ethical Suicides back during our string of interim governments.

"Not much there when you go looking . . . Loosen up, I can see your shoulders knotting . . . Barely enough information to chew on . . . Breathe. Everything comes from the breathing . . ."

I'd often wondered how a man with such leanings could possibly wind up working where he did. Were his intimations a furtive challenge, a testing?

"This is difficult for us to grasp, but you have to look back, to the sense of powerlessness that got tapped into. People were convinced that government, that the country itself, was broken and couldn't be repaired. They saw an endless cycle of paralysis and decay about which they could do nothing. ES's were not about themselves, they were about something much larger."

I stopped to catch breath and shake muscles loose. Took the water bottle from Abraham. Eager electrolytes swarmed within. "Absolute altruism? In addition to which, they acted knowing their actions would come to nothing?"

"That's how it looks to us. To them, who can say? Can we ever appraise the time in which we act?" Abraham stacked virtual weights on the upper-body pulleys, thought a moment and dialed it down a notch. "You're skeptical."

"Of more and more every day."

"With good reason." He reached for the water bottle at the very moment I held it out. *Another dead soldier* had become a joke between us.

Shortly thereafter, as had become our custom, sheathed in featherweight warmsuits, we were walking the grounds. Snow still fell, but lightly, haltingly. "When I first came, not so many years ago," Abraham said, "there were still dove in the trees, calling to one another. It was the loneliest sound I'd ever heard."

The rehab facility had originated at city's edge, adjacent to a cemetery with old religious and older racial divisions, then, as the city burgeoned, found itself ever closer to center. The cemetery was gone, doves too, but bordering stands of trees and dense growth remained.

Farther in toward the heart of the complex sat the original building about which all else had accrued, three stories of rust-colored brick facade and clear plastic windows that on late evenings caught up the sun's light to transform it into swirling, ungraspable, ghostlike figures. Other times, passing by, I'd look up to see those within, on the second floor, peering out, and feel a pull at something deep inside myself, an uneasiness for which I had neither word nor explanation.

It was Abraham who took me there late one night. *The colony*, as he put it, *is sleeping, nessun dorma.* Entering, we passed up narrow stairs and along a corridor with indirect lighting set low in the walls, then to a single door among dozens. There was a scarred window in the door and in the window, still as a portrait in its frame, a face.

"This is Julie," Abraham said.

The woman's face turned slightly as though to locate the sound of his voice. Her eyes behind the glass were cloudy and unfocused. They didn't move, didn't see. After a moment she shuffled back away from the door, obviously in pain, perhaps remembering what had happened other times when voices came and the door opened.

"Surely you must have known," Abraham said. "You had to suspect."

That scientific advances do not happen without experimentation, and that experimentation walks hand in hand with failure?

So much gone deeply wrong with this woman, so many failures in the world that put her there.

9.

Most of the rest you know, or a version of it. You live in a world formed by the rest. You also believe you had some say in the making of that world, I suspect, and I suppose you did, but it was a small say, three or four words lost to a crowded page. There's a long line of wizards behind the curtain vying for their turn at the wheel. When Fran and I floated to the top one more time before sinking out of sight for good, whatever grand intentions might have been packed away in our luggage, truthfully we were doing little more than the wizards' work. Can we ever appraise the time in which we act? Probably not. How do we decide? With a wary smile and fingers crossed.

It was Abraham who called out to me, and to others like me with whom he had worked over the years. Abraham, who once carried me across the room as though I could walk, to qualify me for rehab. Abraham who never hesitates to remind us that we stagger from place to place, day to day, beneath the moral weight of acts we didn't commit but for which we are responsible. That in allowing ourselves collectively to think certain thoughts we risk damaging, even destroying, the lives of millions, yet surely, if any of this means anything at all, we must be free to think those thoughts, to think *all* thoughts.

Never forget it's because of such men as Abraham and Merritt Li that you have the life you do, with its fundamental rights and fail-safes.

Try always to remember the responsibility that comes with those freedoms.

The easy part of government? Ideals. Rational benevolence.

The hardest? Avoiding the terrible gravity of bureaucracy, the pull away from service toward self-survival.

Max Weber had it right over a century ago.

Not much time left for me now. What came to the fore in that Alaska safe house has run its course. I can feel systems shutting down one by one, like lights going off sequentially from room to room, hallway to hallway. The overloaded wire burning down. I'm intrigued by how familiar it feels, how welcome, a visit from an old friend.

Fran is here waiting with me.

Opposite my bed there's a window that for a long while I took to be a link screen as in it I watched people come and go, out in the world, I thought. Couples strolling, crowds flowing off platforms and onto trains, scenes of towns like Claeton, like those in Oregon. Children playing. But that couldn't be right, could it?

I am eight. I have no idea as yet how much heartache is in the world, how much pain, how it goes on building, day by day. I have a new toy, a two-tier garage made of tin, with ramps and tiny pumps and service pits, and I'm running my truck from one to another, making engine sounds, brake sounds, happy driver sounds. On a TV against the wall at room's end, videos of war machines flanked by infantry unspool as a government official inset upper left reads from a prompter saying that high-level talks are underway and that we expect—

And that can't be right either. I'm imagining this, surely, not the garage, the garage was real, but the crash of that newscast into my reverie . . . Am I dreaming? It's harder and harder to tell memory from dream, imaginings from hallucination. Harder and harder, too, to summon much concern which is which, to believe it matters.

All in a moment I am that child with his garage, I am pulling myself along with impossible arms after the toxins take over, I am struggling to stand and stay upright in rehab once brought home from the battlefield and yet again after the surgery, I am driving deserted highways at 10:36 on Union Day.

Fran leans close, her hand on mine. I see but cannot feel it. As she will not hear the last thing I tell her. That we go on and on and, all the time, terrible engines whirl and crash about us, in the great empty spaces that surround our lives.

CARRIERS

"To live past the end of your myth is a perilous thing."

—Anne Carson

PART ONE

1.

Soldiers came up the gully late that afternoon. Even to the kids who lived there—Kelly was twelve then, Eric was sixteen—they looked young. And the word *soldiers* came to them the way most words did those days, loose and slippery so they didn't stay around too long. The troop's uniforms were tatters, pieced together from rags and recommissioned cast-offs. The fact that they got around to this stray patch of land at all meant the government must already have won over or rounded up everyone else. In the scheme of things Kelly and Eric didn't matter. They were stragglers, leftovers, leavings.

But then, if this was part of any regular army, it could also mean the machine was running down.

In any real contest, whatever grand ideas one may

have, next to food those ideas come up short and, from the look of the troops, it had been a while. The runt of the litter found the kids' stock of canned food, opened one of green beans and ate them cold out of the can. Another came across a pot of boiled crawfish that had been on the stove at least three days, dug through the crust of congealed fat and pulled out parts of bodies with his fingers.

Minutes after downing the can of beans, small fry was honking up his guts over by the tree line. Despite this, they raided the kids' food stock and loaded what was left of it aboard an ancient pickup the color of clay and of the smoke pouring from it before loading the kids on.

The soldiers tied the kids' waists with grimy ropes, and tied the ropes to rings set into the floor of the truck bed. One of them, the one with a shotgun, sat back there with them. Tattoos of American flags and naked women covered his left arm. As the truck pulled away, Eric watched a deer step from the trees and begin eating what the runt had thrown up.

After that, he must have dozed off. He woke to find his sister and the kid soldier side by side. She was playing coy, he was snuggling up ever closer. Then—with a flash of reflected light—Kelly had the knife he'd worn on his belt. The boy made a grab for the shotgun on the truck bed beside him, then slumped back. Blood bubbled out around the hilt of the knife in his neck as he breathed. Eric worked at his ropes.

The one in the passenger seat up front twisted around to look as the driver hit the brakes hard. Kelly was over the side, rolling, then up and running for the trees. The passenger-side door flew open so fast it rebounded against him as the soldier raised his rifle. He got off a single shot before Eric was on top of him, riding momentum and body weight to take him down, pounding away at him. He heard another shot and looked up to see Kelly fall. She'd almost made it to the tree line. The driver was swinging his rifle around toward Eric just as the shotgun's load hit him in the chest.

Kelly died soon after. Eric was there with her, beside her, the way he had been their whole lives. She couldn't talk, but their eyes held. He watched as the pain went out of them. She was the brave one, Eric thought, the one who took after Mom and Dad, rebellion and hopes for a better world in her bone and in her blood. Not him. He'd always been more a mind-my-own-business, get-by sort.

When she was gone, Eric went over to make sure the soldiers were, too.

2.

You keep your head down. You attend to the work assigned you. There's not much sense to any of it, of course, but if you fail to survive there's even less.

You do what you can. The rest, all you can't do, can't accomplish, you carry around with you.

Mary Jean Lovegirl was born, she likes to say, on Union Day. Unlikely, but that's the story. We see her every few weeks. Broken bones, beatings, malnutrition, the latest strain of virus trying for a foothold. Treat and street. With ever diminishing funds, insufficient staff and makeshift supplies, we're hard pushed to accomplish even that.

Years back, when I understood, I would have explained it to you. Governments form tribally, to protect one group from another. As government evolves, protection turns inward, toward protecting the weaker among the group itself. But in time the overseers come to believe that stability can reside solely with them; the first order of business becomes holding their position.

It's a curious sort of infection and, years later, I was part of the defense, one cell among antibodies flooding in to challenge it, little suspecting that I myself hosted a similar infection. Both are history now. My supposed great efforts are laid to rest. I don't recruit, lecture or train people anymore, I don't set bombs or know those who do, I don't destroy data. I can no longer summon whatever it would take to believe I understand.

The hardest thing is standing by, *palliative* ringing like aftershock in your ear and always on your mind, thinking *If only*, fully aware there are drugs and treatments that might save them, that would at the very least diminish pain and suffering, drugs and treatments to which you have no access. Somehow you've become a frontier doctor, treating cancer with hacksaws and dressmaker's thread. You try not to think overmuch how the ruins of a city, the ruins of a nation, the ruins of your profession, are piled up around you.

You do what you can. The rest, you carry around.

This afternoon, as I'm cleaning out an infected gash that runs half the length of Mary Jean's thigh, four police appear at the front door and call for papers. They're uniformed in the new fashion and look like soldiers. Patients deeper in the waiting room begin to thin out. They know where back exits are. Two near the entrance have no papers to hand over and are stood against the wall. One trooper, twice the age of his counterparts at least, attends them. You wonder at the action he must have seen over the years, what he must think of all this. He's from a different world than the others, he's witnessed everything spin out of control, wobble back in and break down again and again. Time was, you could have seen what he's been through in his eyes, but it's sunk deep now. You can't see it down there. Maybe he couldn't even find it if he went looking.

This time there's no personal challenge. The leader comes up close to see what I'm doing but after a moment nods and steps away without demanding my papers or Mary Jean's. These particular troopers haven't been here before. Some units are formal, straight-backed, even stiffly polite, others reek of cruelty and damage. You never know.

They're still working their way along the line when the leader punches into his link and holds up a hand. Everyone waits. We're out and about, men, he says. Called off to something else, something bigger, maybe real, maybe not. Could be a fire, another building collapse, some official on the move. Could just as well be resisters staging a diversion to pull police away, or simply to cause confusion. The cells are ragtag nowadays, but they're still there and they still function, sometimes independently, sometimes in concert. The police are every bit as ragtag. Mostly young, put out on the streets with minimal training, overfills of youthful anger, surfeits of gear and firepower, and a knowledge of history that would fit into one of their utility pockets.

Whatever the provenance of the callout, we take it as gift and go about our work, wading into the standard run of malnutrition, chronic infection, addiction, opportunistic disease, congenital disorders, ever more manifest aftereffects from chemical and neurological agents deployed in the Seven Day Wars. Early afternoon, on an amputee, I encounter a fungus of a type I haven't before. Not long after, with the waiting room beginning to show empty chairs, I take a break to gear down and recover blood sugar. Lying on a table in the back, slow regular breathing, cracks snapping along my spine. I've eaten cheese and an apple. My link's on low. I reach down, locate it by feel and thumb up the volume, more to mask the din from outside than anything else. I do my best to stay away from news, but sometimes it finds you anyway. I learn that yet again there will be no funds dedicated to rebuilding the highway system and the power plants that are fritzing out one by one like ancient light bulbs, or to reopening schools and hospitals, as various government factions spar and vie for top jock.

Relaxing for a few minutes is one thing, falling asleep quite another. I indulged in both then came awake, instantly as always, to someone stepping quietly away, half aware of a presence above but moments ago. I'd been climbing stairs soundlessly, age twelve, with no idea where I might be headed, passing through checkpoint after checkpoint being asked questions in languages I'd never before heard.

"You need me?"

Abend turned back. "And *you* need the rest."

"We all do. What is it?"

"Possible critical injury. Acute infection for sure. Susan's elbow-deep in a flail chest."

Same as me, Susan went through med school hanging onto the fraying safety net of a government with the will (inconstant) and resources (withering) to provide for the well-being of its citizens. Off we went at that government's expense, both of us twice the age of others in the class. Susan earned her place with years of teaching biological sciences. I'd put in eight as a self-trained medic for one of the most impoverished city-states. Read up on emergency and support care, took the test, got my certificate. The training I got in med school wasn't much more comprehensive. They pushed us through as fast as they could.

As Abend and I headed to the exam room, he filled me in. Late adolescent male, multiple abrasions, lacerations, general bruising, ugly hematoma on the back of his neck, deep gash, severe infection.

"He didn't come in by himself, not like that."

"Guy staying at the same overnight brought him in. Temp's hanging around one-oh-three, one-oh-four. He's pretty much out of it."

"Staph?"

"Staph, MRSA, viral—anyone's guess what's growing in there. Nasty, whatever it is. And it's got a good hold. I pulled samples for the lab when I drew blood."

"Structural damage with the neck trauma?"

"None that I can see or palpate. X-ray's down again."

"Of course it is. You started antibiotics?"

"That's going to have to be your call, Doc, low as our stocks are."

Our patient was on his side, propped with folded blankets to take pressure off neck and upper back and keep his head straight. Another, presumably the man who brought him in from the overnight, sat on a metal stool nearby. That one's eyes met mine and held half a beat longer than they should have.

I poked and prodded, swabbed and sniffed, leaned close for the best look I could get. Abend and I cleaned the wound, stitched it loosely in the likely case we'd need to reopen, field-dressed it. I signed for the antibiotics.

"And get that X-ray when the machine comes back up."

"You mean if," Abend said. "Like us, the machines do eventually give out."

"And ours has been doing so for a long time. We have a name for this young man?"

"Nothing. No papers, nothing of a personal nature on him." We both looked up at the other man, who shook his head.

"I don't think the clothes were his. Way off size."

"Provided by a shelter?"

"Or stolen."

"Best get prints and scans to Central, then. When you get the chance."

"In due time, doctor. As per regulation. Of course."

I steered back toward the break room but got reined in before I went ten steps. Susan's flail chest was coding. Her patient had been brought in by one of the self-appointed neighborhood patrols. They'd found her out behind the old public library now become a shelter, attacked for who knows what reason, if any at all, or by whom, given the countless furies brewing and breaking out on every side. We worked for fifteen, twenty minutes before calling it. Coding's something we rarely do, and I don't know what prompted Susan's decision, but once it tips that way, you go all out, throw in everything you have.

The next shift got in late due to a shutdown on the central line, so it was full nighttime before I could break away. Made sure I had my curfew pass and papers close at hand.

I got less than a block before being joined. He emerged from a crevice between buildings and fell in stride straightaway.

"Your man in there get those scans sent?"

"It's been busy. Possibly he overlooked it."

"There's always tomorrow." Half a block more went by. "Good to see you, Anton. Imagine my surprise."

"That we're both still alive?"

"Lives don't turn out close to the way we think, do they?"

"Not much does."

"True . . ." For a moment I felt his attention shift. Implants, I assumed. Listening. "The boy's name is Eric. Nineteen years old. He was living as small as it gets, huddled down close to the ground and every dark corner he could find. Grabbed off the street by one of the neighborhood watch groups, maybe, or by troops—who knows? Eric made it to the overnight before he collapsed. One of ours found him there."

"And brought him here."

"By chance." Eli stopped walking and glanced

ahead. “Police set up a new checkpoint three blocks north.”

“I take it your people have upgraded their toys.”

“They get better signal fires, we get better spotters. I’d best not be here. Perhaps another nine years won’t pass before we meet again.”

3.

That's where it would have ended, but I arrived the next morning to find Eric gone, taken by soldiers during the night. The night nurse who tried to intervene now lay on his gurney with two cracked ribs and a probable concussion. X-ray was still down. When she asked for cause, she said, they ignored her. When she insisted, two of them pushed her down and kicked her. A patient on a nearby gurney, probable stomach cancer, said some of the soldiers "slurred words together the way they do over in Clarkston" where she was born, and were talking among themselves about the boy being a longtime fugitive. Like we all aren't, she added.

They'd come in before to scoop up young men and women for conscription—easy pickings, after all—but those were essentially healthy specimens and not beat halfway into coma. Which made one wonder if the boy, Eric, had something they wanted. They must have thought so. Hard to figure what that might be. Knowledge? Information? Skills? None seemed likely, from what Eli told me of the boy's keeping low and loose.

In following days I did my best to stay low and loose myself, half expecting further intrusions at any time. The city, meanwhile, was oddly quiet. Walking home nights, I'd spot gangs on prowl or on patrol, depending on one's point of view, and give them wide berth. Even then it was an open secret that the government lent active support to the gangs. There were never enough troops or police, and in the aspirant statist's handbook, as in the revolutionary's, the first step always is to spread disorder, to destabilize.

Saturday about a week later, another of those fourteen-hour days, I stopped off at a bodega for milk on my way home. The clerk looked to be startled when I came through the door. The shelves didn't have much on them. The only milk in the cooler had expired days ago and was a brand I'd never seen or heard of. When I asked the clerk where it was from, he shrugged and said one of the towns next border over, they took what they could get, which wasn't much. And so did I.

That same night, a group of bedraggled soldiers

came off the train at Fullerton Square as I passed with my bag of mystery milk. By then we'd all lost count how many wars we were fighting, some of them with or against fledgling nations close enough to our own that troops periodically could commute home and back. I couldn't help but think how startling the sight of men in uniforms with multiple weapons striding among the general population once would have been.

Within days the streets came alive again, flash marches, demonstrations and protests popping up all over, police responding. Official news concerned itself with newly signed treaties, puff pieces on Chief Administrator Derek and feel-good human interest stories. I concerned myself with getting through the days at the clinic. It's never so much dealing with one crisis after another as it is learning to step lightly across, as on rolling logs, as they surface. Getting to the other side is what you do.

Thoughts turned back to the clinic's need for supplies, stalled requests for same, the steady reappearance of diseases once all but eradicated: tuberculosis, opportunistic infections, even smallpox. Poor diet, spotty medical care, population density and inadequacies of water and sanitation facilities will do that. Not to mention lack of inoculations or, for that matter, access to vaccines.

Another late night then, and those of us on the streets were wearing bright yellow curfew passes clipped to outer garments when, as I turned a corner, Eli stepped from a doorway.

"Come with me."

"Absolutely not."

"Please," he said, and at his gesture two others stepped into half-light.

I nodded.

Taking a long stagger of side streets, cross-unders and walkways, we ended up in a warehouse at city's edge, which from the look of it even vermin had long since abandoned. Eli led me into a room fitted out as an operating theater. The boy Eric lay on one of the tables. His eyes were dull, but alert.

"I apologize," Eli said. "Our own physicians would have dealt, but six nights ago they were taken by authorities. He needs attention."

I settled in to cleaning, stitching, probing. Within the hour, I was done with what could be done. When I looked up, two bags of IV antibiotics lay on the stand by me. Such as were always in short supply at the clinic, unavailable for months at the time.

"There's more. Whatever you need," Eli said. As I started the IV and hung bags, he went on. "The boy was being held at a blind spot government facility. Something brought on a shutdown of systems—a hack? a glitch? power loss? We don't know. But it went on long enough for Eric to escape."

"Impressive, considering the condition he's in."

"He comes from tough stock. Raised in the backwoods of Louisiana. Hunting, fishing, living off the land. Eating fish, frogs, stewed weeds—who knows? Off screen, out of sight, all his life."

"Till now. Till he caught the government's eye."

"There isn't a government, Anton. Pure illusion. What we have are factions, six of them, eight, each one working chiefly to consolidate power, aggrandize itself, then push through some recondite agenda for social order. Eric had agendas of his own. He killed those who came into the woods and bayous after him."

"Soldiers?"

"Of a sort."

"And he wants back in the shadows?"

"Where he lives, yes. The killing didn't stop with those who first came after him. It continued here, for much the same reasons."

Which explained the soldiers' interest.

For a moment I thought I could hear whispers from Eli's implant, then realized it was the man and woman who had come along with us and who now stood across the room by the door quietly talking.

"Eric wasn't alone in taking advantage of the systems failure," Eli said. "Our dragliners caught on immediately to what was happening. When systems started back up, they were ready for it, hopscotched their way in. So now we have new back doors."

Eli's people guided me back to the central city, after which I made it home with a single stop for papers and pass verification. There, I fell into bed for just over four hours of something more akin to suspended animation than sleep, completely disoriented when the link pinged me awake at my usual time, thrashing my way up like a half-drowned man to the surface.

As I stood eating oatmeal, early light moving away from me across the floor, I learned there had been an attempted military coup just before dawn, police, soldiers and security forces all milling about in this grand clash where no one could tell who was what and which side they might be on.

As I stopped by to check on my latest patient, having committed the route to memory on my way home, I found the warehouse entrance open, no one about, Eric again gone missing. On the floor of the treatment room among ungathered detritus from my efforts last night, gauze pads, bandages, Betadine and alcohol packets, a rubber tourniquet, lay Eli's body.

I FIRST MET ELI in the coffee shop across from the university. When I went to take his order I noticed how, where he sat by the windows, late afternoon light fell onto his table, one side bright, the other in shadow, and took note as well of the book he read: *A History of Radical Thought*. Later I'd wonder if the book might have been bait of a sort.

I knew that book pretty well.

Eight credits short of my degree, I was pulling down the coffeehouse gig two days a week for free food and pocket change while interning part-time, with precious little training and still less awareness of the responsibilities I'd shouldered, as a juvie officer for kids scant years younger than myself.

Soon Eli and I together rode gritty, forever-late trains, drank coffee or stalked city streets on our way to meetings, deep in the sort of conversations that get dropped then picked up the next time exactly where you left off. I must have got on fairly soon to the fact that I was being recruited.

That flame in his eye—ambition or passion? Whatever it was, it was contagious, moving again and again into new hosts and taking hold. He was brilliant at what he did, brilliant at what he believed, and through him, because of him, we all burned a bit brighter ourselves.

"There's only so much of anything in the world, Anton," he'd say. "Material resources, wealth, water, land. The question's always how it will be distributed. And there's no correct answer."

Or: "Some want to change the world, believe it can be made better, whether by increments or radical upset. Others want to hold it still, to *keep* it from changing. And a few long only to tear it up, burn it down."

I've long thought of my function here as that of scribe, of amanuensis, scribbling history on the walls of the cave, doing my unskilled best to copy down portions of what I've seen. But maybe I'd best be considered a translator. Here's my version, the translator says. I've done what I can to be true to the original. Sorry so much gets lost.

IN AN ALLEY NEAR the warehouse I found a second body, the man who killed Eli, I assumed, pursued and brought to rest by Eric.

Eric himself showed up shortly after, as I rounded a corner. Still afoot, but barely. Wounds had reopened. He was pale and shaky from blood loss, breathing hard and shallow. Drenched with sour-smelling sweat.

There was nothing to do but take him back to my apartment, thinking the whole time we would never make it. Luckily it was a quiet morning, with few patrols on the streets, and I did my best to keep Eric out of direct sight of those, and of scanners. Got him settled in on the daybed, raided emergency supplies I kept at home, and patched him up again as he slept. I linked the clinic to let them know I'd be there shortly, left a message for Eric that would trigger when he started moving around the room, and arrived at work painfully late to find the power out. Been out most of the morning, Rickett told me. Links were saying four hours more.

We coped as best we could. Ever try removing a cast with a box cutter? Cauterizing a wound with an open flame? And never mind that when you're working in an old warehouse space there's not much window and ambient light. We'd partitioned off the floor with jerry-built low walls. Never before had I seen so many heads popping over the top of them like prairie dogs, looking around either to see if everyone else was having as much trouble as they were or to find out what others were doing that might work better.

And the blackout was seven hours, not four.

The wife of a suicidal man I treated following his third failed attempt told me she never knew what she'd be coming home to. She'd try to shake it off during the day, attend to her work, but it was always there at the back of her mind, that thought. Which is how I felt making my way home that night. More suspecting what I'd find than wondering, really, and I was right.

Eric was gone. He'd tagged onto the message I left him that morning, thanking me and apologizing for taking with him the painkillers in my emergency stash. *Figure I'll need them*, his note read.

WRITING ALL THAT DOWN now, I feel what a history teacher must feel telling young children about a world so distant from theirs that they can't imagine it, let alone, even for a moment, inhabit it.

Here's the shape I thought my life would have: I'd top-score SATs, hit college running with majors in a couple of humanities, acquire a master's, push on to a PhD, pass my years sitting in a small office, departing occasionally to teach, travel home and back, or attend a faculty meeting as my hair grew ever thinner, doctor's appointments took over my calendar, and I began adding layers of clothing, devising ruse after ruse to cover lapses in memory.

Back as early as age twelve I started to wonder if in some sense we don't all live by slogans, fully believing we've chosen them, too rarely understanding that they've been foisted upon us, as often by ourselves as by others. This is who I am, we'd say. Then: Property is theft, Less government is best government, Trust in the Lord to guide you, Every man a king, A chicken in every pot, From each according to his ability to each according to his need.

I became accustomed to lifting up the flap of the words we live by and looking beneath.

My brother Saul was beside me in the Red April marches where police, in a nod to ancient tradition, put away their stunners and rubber bullets and stepped out with truncheons, one of which caught Saul on the back of the head. He came awake hours later with virtually no memory, cognitive powers that flickered and flared out for the rest of his life, with just enough sure function to feed and dress himself and follow lists of activities posted each morning on the kitchen link screen.

Six years and half as many governments after the marches, at the end of a long string of good days, good weeks in fact, Saul died of a massive overdose. I suppose it was those good weeks that made it possible for him to plan and carry out such action. He'd squirreled away pain killers, barbiturates, muscle relaxants, whatever came to hand, and early one afternoon ate them all—by the fistful, one has to imagine. With so little fine muscle control remaining, Saul had been unable to write for years. On the kitchen table, held in place by his favorite cup, he left a sheet of paper. Painstakingly glued to it, almost straight, were words he'd cut from computer printouts, just like kidnappers demanding ransom in the old movies he loved. *No more*, the note said, *I'm sorry. No more.*

Today we're on track, tomorrow our lives go skittering off and we pick up the pace, sprinting hard so as not to be left behind.

That night, I remember, the night Eric disappeared for what I thought a final time, I had the dream again. Having tracked it at last to its lair, I confronted the monster. A female, I realized. Just as I fired, she turned to one side to make of herself a smaller target and I saw the baby clutched to her breast, suckling. I could never remember what happened to the baby once the monster died. Did it die also? Starve to death slowly afterward? Survive? I went over the events of the dream again and yet again in my mind, but could never get past the monster lying there, right hand cradling the child, left hand scrabbling at the floor as though to hold onto this world seconds longer, a world that had become immeasurably precious.

4.

Years would pass, just over a dozen, time itself as fluid as memory, before we'd meet again, years in which I came to wonder if ours might not be the only country ever to colonize and recolonize itself.

Incrementally, unexpectedly, even violently, we change, as does the world. Did I recognize the nation upon which I opened blinds that morning? Barely. Did I recognize myself? Most days, no. The old Anton, the old nation, they were both in there somewhere. We think we've left used-up lives behind, like nail or hair clippings or shells gone too small for hermit crabs, but we've lugged them along with us. Sometimes, long after, we begin to feel a need to hold on to those other times and selves, to set down what remains of them. We even make cursory notes—a scatter of highlights—to that end.

—Thoughts I had as I entered a nondescript room on the second floor of a blank-faced building set behind a complex of administration buildings. Slab steel conference table, molded plastic chairs, pitchers of water on the table, a coffee urn in one corner, mugs with some character to them, fissures, chips, stains. Character lines and cracks in those seated about the table as well, three women, five men.

"I think we can all agree the trains are not running on time," Chief Minister Warren had announced in her link calling us together. *Nothing* was running on time. And some things, including power, water, sanitation services, food supplies and link chains, weren't running at all, or ran intermittently. The water smelled of decay and of chlorine, sewage was backing up into the city's canals, riots had become commonplace, scores of contagions were stomping their way through the populace. Whoever was in the driver's seat had jumped out and left the door open. Often in such power vacuums, the military steps in. Or the police—in our case, it had become increasingly difficult to tell the two apart. This meeting was a last-ditch stand if not to right the ship of state, then at very least to keep it afloat.

Conciliation. Coalition. Call it what you will.

Loye Warren and Karyl Singh stood in for the

government then in power, such as it was. Two were from that government's staunchest opposition, one from a cobbled-together federation of Marxist groups, the military represented by an army general who chose to attend in fatigues, as though the moment we adjourned he'd be back hard at work. I was there, not particularly at my own volition or choice, never a card-carrying believer, as spokesman for a progressive party that of late had taken on weight. If sometimes the party fumbled at finding things to advocate rather than decry, nonetheless it slogged away in good faith, understanding that civilization consists largely of helping one another stop in time.

One left, then.

Eric.

Which put us squarely in what-the-hell territory. I had no idea what others might or might not know of his past, even less idea how he came to be here.

Hardly a come-see-conquer as it turned out, but of all the ways that meeting could have gone, it went the most unlikely: to consensus. By late afternoon an interim government got established, one with serious underpinnings and a gambler's chance at stability. Maybe not real, maybe fool's gold, but hey, it was shiny, and in the circumstances shiny looked good.

"Nothing turned out much the way we thought

it might," Eric said afterward as, tucked close against the river's curves, we walked a narrow, high levee.

"Very little the world's not seen before, though."

"True."

Barges out on the water approached one another from opposite directions and sounded horns. Defunct for half a century, water transportation had made a strong comeback.

Our blather went on a bit, but that's the gist of it, the backbone. Nothing to see here. No password to take you to a true world beneath that of appearance. Nothing to pull it all together, to change your life. No portraits of great men moving against the backdrop of history. Only these two indistinct human voices for a short while, a very short while, resounding.

WE WOKE THE NEXT morning to find ourselves at war.

Not the endless back-burner wars to which we'd grown accustomed, wars that went on long after they passed from newcasts and from our thoughts, but those of the full-bore, flat-out, burn-it-to-the-ground type. Press gangs roamed the earth. The poor, young and unprotected went missing. All about us, terrible engines revved. Rationing, want and hunger were our countrymen. Then, with ongoing failures in sanitation, disease.

So much for our proud consensus.

You know all this, of course. Yet something within me still harbors a faint belief that if only I set this down, I can fix it in memory, or if not in memory, then in some inchoate understanding—can at least, for myself, give it form and shape.

I'd soon be returning to my role as repairman, as physician, again the makeshift doc back on the frontier, doing what I could to stem the damage as humankind turned and turned again in the grave it has so stubbornly been making for itself all its brief years on this earth.

PART TWO

Ghost says someone is coming. Ghost is usually right.

Clouds hang low today, as though sunlight itself were pushing them downward, and the morning mist is slower than usual to dispel. Moments ago, a ragged flock of geese flew over. On their way to better-paying jobs up north, Ghost would say, lodged as he is in his world of the 1800s, able to understand this one only through what he remembers of the other.

Thanks to hunters who last week found their way here from the woods above Atchafalaya, I'm having smoked venison for breakfast this morning. Can't imagine how they did that, or why. I'd traded a stack of furs, some jerked fish and hemp rope for the meat, and was enjoying it with my first mug of mud-thick coffee, when I realized Ghost was there.

The troop had been quite a sight, old jeans and off-size boots, a mess of hats and caps, canvaswear—the last liberated from abandoned hunting lodges, I figured. City folk gone dingo. Look past beards and set jaws, you saw how young they were. Probably everyone looks young nowadays. Pure conjecture, since I haven't seen anyone else in—what? A year? Two? Time's as empty as a taxman's face down here, no reason to track it.

But mornings here come on pure and strong. Everything pushing hard, without and within. There's wonder to it, and there's pain.

And now there's Ghost.

A couple hours, he says. Boat's up past the big bend, moving this way. I don't ask him how he knows this stuff any longer. He can't tell me. But—two hours. Time enough to spiff up the place some, get ready for company. I could wipe off tables and chairs, scrape dried mud off the floor by the door. Put up some nice curtains. Throw some extra lime in the outhouse, at least.

Or I could just sit here, finish my breakfast, and listen to Ghost tell me how battles went, in his day. Ain't nobody came back all right, he says, not ever. Every last one of them, from fourteen-year-old kids to grown men who might of fathered four or six kids theirselves, they'd show back up home and pieces'd be missing, even those that looked okay. Like if you were to build a house without doors, or a roof or floor that worked or one whole side.

Ghost was here when I returned, couldn't tell me how long. *Ever since*, was what he said. From the way he talked of battles, I figured he must have died in the swamps, in some conflict or another. Maybe the dead can't range far from where they fell. And maybe I shouldn't generalize, since he's the only one I've ever met.

But he was right, this time like all the other times. I watched the boat come around that last jutty of trees four hundred meters upriver. A fishing boat, outboard motor of middling power from the sound of it, single occupant. Five meters offshore, unsure of the bottom, he cut the motor, swung it up and coasted in. Stepped off into mud and scummy water without the least hesitation, hauling the boat to ground.

"Forgive the intrusion." He coiled the bow rope and stowed it aboard before looking around. Took in the cabin, the table and chairs set out under a tree halfway to the water, boat dock built of axe-cut cypress. "What the hell year is this?" Furrows on his face were deep, as though gouged, skin so varied in color and texture that it looked patchwork. Mine had to be much the same. I'd seen my last mirror the day I left people and their societies behind.

"This place is harder to find than black hats at midnight." Bird calls had fallen silent as he came around the jutty. Now, as they started up again, he heard. "Your alarm system's back online."

"Not much call for doctors in these parts," I said.

"And some time since I thought of myself as such. The administration and I failed to reach an understanding. I fell out with it. *By* it would be more accurate."

"Which administration?"

"I lost count."

"And here I took you for the bottom-line sort, get the good work done despite."

"So did I, for a long enough time."

"Out here the custom's to offer food. Nothing special, and it for damn sure won't look like much. But it'll do. And you have to be hungry, it's a long ride. Plus, I owe you. For sewing me up. For the pain meds."

I held up a hand.

"Come on to the cabin while I pull stuff together. Can't leave anything out down here. If birds and bugs don't get it, an alligator's sure to waddle up out of the bayou and snag it."

Soon we were back out at the table, steam rising from coffee mugs and clouds of mosquitos hovering about as we reminisced. We'd spent what, maybe six hours together, all told? All those years ago. So there weren't a lot of shiny stones to pull out of the basket and hold up. We worked with what we had. I thanked him for his care, told him I'd recovered to carry on with what I'd been doing.

"I heard," Doc said. "Do you have any idea how many officials you eliminated, how many cruelties and how much damage you may have curbed?"

"Not near as many or much as I got credit for."

"All in the day's work of a folk hero."

"Yet in the end . . ." He fell silent. Listening, alert. "Someone else is here," he said. "You're not alone."

GHOST SAYS HE LONG believed if he talked about things he'd lose them, they'd go away and he'd never get them back. So he kept it all to himself. I don't ask for how long. As far as I can tell, Ghost has no sense of time, there's only this eternal present.

Ghost's initial appearance came not as one might imagine, at night, but in early morning hours, mist rolling low on the water, me with a cup of stovetop coffee (boil water, throw coffee in, turn off the fire) down by the boat. Sensing I wasn't alone, I turned and there he was.

Unaccountably, the first words from my mouth were "Waiting long?" to which he replied "A while." Soon enough it became apparent that, as far as chronology was concerned, *A while* did for all. How long have you been here? A while. Were you here when I first came back? A while.

His stories were as much a mystery as his chronology, bits and pieces thrown together into a stewpot from which lumps, one here, another there, got picked out.

His parents were, I think, from some of his remarks, foreigners—immigrants. Comments suggest that quite early on he participated in large-scale battles, perhaps a war or series of such. When this may have occurred, what country or side he may have served, or how long this went on, I've no idea. Other stories cause me to wonder if he may have been interred in some manner of holding facility, perhaps as a prisoner of war, perhaps in a civil prison once fighting ceased. Maybe it's there he died.

Once that first morning I asked if he often thought about dying, how it felt. Like taking the next breath, he said. A long one.

DAYLIGHT HAD BARELY GONE ripe when Larson called out *Bone jour!* from forest's edge. This is what passes for wit from neighbor Larson, his being every bit as Cajun as the mosquitos and dragonflies that surround us and as adept at humor as, say, Disraeli. Doc and I stepped outside.

"This one yours?" Larson said.

He had beside him a man maybe twenty years younger than myself, hands rope-tied, looking quite the worse for wear.

"Came across this one's boat just upstream." While out hunting, no doubt. "Came across him minutes later, boy ain't spent a day out some town his whole life. Snaking right along, he must of thought, never once took note how everything around'm went quiet."

Doc and I exchanged glances. He shook his head.

"You don't want him," Larson said. "I can toss him in the water and be done with."

I said since he'd gone to all this trouble we might as well keep the boy and asked Larson if he'd stay for coffee, but he said he'd best get back. He walked to the tree line, was there, then was gone. "We all run tight schedules out here," I told Doc.

We propped our guest up on a chair inside. He sat looking around, at cockeyed windows, gaps where walls once met, floor planks worn smooth and sway-back, wilderness and green water out front, smell of bodies and earth in here, wondering what the hell kind of world he had got himself into. Doc took a chair across from him while I started the coffee.

"I don't know you," Doc said.

The man met his eyes full on but said nothing.

"Yet you followed me here."

Again silence.

"Are you Union—"

"No!"

Whatever the word for which Doc intended *Union*

as modifier, it got lost. The man's denial came so fast that the two words, *union* and *no*, sounded as one.

In the distance I heard what I was sure was a small plane. Surely they weren't flying again? How long had it been?

"There are groups of us—" the man said.

"Cells."

"On our own. Separately. We know how mutable, how labile, history can be. We think it's important to hear what took place from those who were present."

"Ah, youth," Doc said into the hush that followed. "Forever looking to change the world, or to save it."

Our visitor held up his bound hands. "Could we forego the rope? Having come all this way, I'm unlikely to flee now."

I grabbed a knife and cut him loose. Still a few fish scales on the blade.

He thanked us and met Doc's eyes. "I spent most of a year searching for you. Your old neighborhoods, places you worked. In the course of it I came across a man who'd been seriously injured in the aftermath of a police raid. He'd been given emergency treatment by a bystander at the scene who immediately fled, someone I came to believe, as I questioned the man further, might be you. I got closer and closer, and when I got right up next to you, you were already on your way here. I had to ask what would impel you to make such a journey."

His attention shifted to me.

"I had no idea who that would be," he said. "How could I?"

"This matters because?"

"The doctor had his reason for coming here."

Doc leaned in a bit. "Tell us, since I myself remain unsure."

"The same as mine, I suspect." Back again, then, to me. "Your actions, what you did, these don't exist in official records."

"It was all covered over. Erased, expunged."

"But people knew—not the details, but they understood something of the changes taking place. Sensed them, saw them. Heard stories, story after story. And that understanding grew."

"None of it made much of a difference," I said. "Moving furniture about a room. You spend hours at it, then you look around and what you see is the same table, chairs, walls. Maybe there's a little more afternoon light, or now you can see that one tree outside."

"Time can change that."

"You're right. It does. Everything. Always."

THAT NIGHT THE VISITOR told us his earliest memories were of running the streets with friends, with others brought up in his part of the city. Like birds that never stray far from their birth tree, he said. There were too many people, too little of everything else. From time to time, randomly, it seemed, government trucks would show up. Standing in the back, soldiers would tip their loads of foodstuff, canned goods, cereal, flatbreads, onto the street. Moving in low and fast, the children grabbed whatever they could and ran, hid their finds, came back for it later.

That night, too, the water was—*alive* is the only word I can find. This sense of quickening, of turns and dives deep within the stillness, as though the water itself were breathing, something you only see when storms are far off and on their way.

Throughout the day, Ghost had been around but kept his distance. I'd spot him off by the trees, watching through the window as we talked, keeping pace as we moved here or there. That night as I stood by water's edge, Doc and visitor asleep inside, he came up beside me.

"You never mentioned you were a soldier," Ghost said.

"I wasn't, not in the sense you mean."

"You fought. You killed."

"Yes."

"Something was that important."

"I believed so."

"In the course of our lives we believe many things."

"Yes."

"What other maps do we have?"

Next morning, the storm came the way storms do

here, slamming in mercilessly all at once, lashing at treetops, blowing open gates to another dimension, another world. Generator down, we found ourselves huddled in the cabin in near darkness. We spoke for a time but proved poor contest to wind and rain so loud that we could scarcely make out what others were saying and at length sat quietly in our own separate spaces of memory and waiting.

Once I asked Ghost if he would be here when we're all gone. I was splitting firewood for the stove, I remember. Late afternoon, new generations of frogs thrumming in the shallows. Ghost stood looking off into stands of oak, bald cypress and tupelo gum and after a moment said he believed not.

THREE DAYS LATER DOC, Ghost and I were hunting mushrooms in the woods. These seemed to have sprung up overnight in the wake of the storm, some the size of human thumbs already, their gills beautifully formed—intricate, and somehow intimate. I put out an arm to hold Doc back as a young cottonmouth slithered through undergrowth directly before us. Mementos of the storm—disembodied branches, Spanish moss ripped from trees, dead fish and small game—lay everywhere. Mud, silt, leaves and other detritus had fetched up against the bases of trees to form mounds that looked like animal dens.

There wasn't much left to be said. Hadn't been a

lot to say in the first place. But if our young historian hadn't got quite what he hoped for, he did have a decent weight of recollections to cart back with him to civilization. And Doc? More than once I'd had the suspicion that he might turn out to be that guest in old stories who came for dinner and just can't bring himself to leave.

And there we were, the two of us, three of us really, no money in our purses and no prospects, grim with wakened memories following wet, stormy days, standing amid galleries of funerals for people we'd known and grand ideals long laid away.

Those who know history understand that the lives of revolution's children do not go well.

THEY LEFT, THE TWO of them, just after daybreak. No tidying up in this account, no stitches and casts and touch-ups. Remnants of the storm were still much in evidence, bayou waters dark and murky, sun heaving itself above the rim of trees. Doc had come out to stand by me earlier as I tossed stale bread and leftovers into the water.

"That's what they gave us, most days," he said. "Bread. Water. The water was foul. You got where you looked forward to the taste of the mold on the bread."

"You were in prison."

"For a time. Not as long as many others."

"I'm sorry."

I finished with the bread and turned back toward the cabin, Doc alongside.

"The one who was with you when I came?" he said.

"Yes?" Ghost, he meant. Doc had sensed his presence early on.

"I hope you'll bid him farewell for me."

"I will."

"And that he proves fair company."

Later, as Doc's boat approached the long curve, as Doc and visitor lifted arms in final goodbyes, Ghost appeared beside me. All this was his, after all, far more than it could ever be any of ours. Contrary to what he said, I believe he will be here once I'm gone. We stood together, Ghost and I, watching silently, as the boat swung past the curve and we could no longer see them, until the world closed around them anew.

SETTLERS

Everything that moves is alive and a threat—a reminder to be as still as possible. Devastation occurs

whether we're paying attention or not. The options: repair a world or build a new one.

—Kaveh Akbar

Donse and I were playing with the eyebox when we heard them coming. Two, maybe three of them, talking among themselves, people unaccustomed to moving about in these parts. We didn't know what the box was, what it did, not really, but when you urged it to life with a gentle shake, something changed inside. There'd be movement, dim figures stirring within the murk. One of the fathers had noticed us with the eyebox yesterday and asked to see it. After a moment he handed it back. This was no toy, he said, this is from before. We knew that, we'd heard what people used to be able to do. How skimmers big and heavy as mountains flew around the world, hundreds at a time. How at the push of a button people's images appeared before you as though they were truly there.

Our jump hole was six meters away from the clearing, where four live oak touched shoulders. Put one foot hard on a corner and a trap opened along the side just enough for a body to roll and slide through. Once it closed up again, it couldn't be seen. Parents had their own jump holes farther up the hollow, away from camp.

We lay there listening to feet crashing through grass and undergrowth as the voices grew louder. The footsteps stopped close by.

"Pretty sure someone's in here," one voice said. We could hear them patting and pulling just above, then light showed around the cover's edge as it got hauled up. Muscles stood out on the man's arms. He was beardless.

"Hello, young man."

Donse and I climbed out just as Father Drew emerged from the tree line. Others would be in the trees with weapons. Donse and I knew that. The newcomers may have known too. The one who'd found our jump hole held both hands up, palms out. "We neither bring harm nor intend to take away what is yours."

Father Drew came closer, little more than a man's length. I heard sounds in the trees as others shifted closer as well. The newcomers gave no sign of having heard.

"It's your skimmers that came over?" Father said.

Three times. Fathers had explained to us what the skimmers were, tiny versions of the old airplanes, canvas over wood frames, with small engines and limited range.

The newcomer, Ahmed as we were soon to learn, nodded.

"Searching," Father Drew said.

"For you, yes. To come and ask if you might allow us to join you."

"Bringing strife, hunger and skirmish along with you as cartage."

"Quite the opposite. Leaving them behind. You came here to survive. We want the same for our families."

"It's gone that bad."

"It's gone unsupportable. Foundations fall away, one after another. Whatever's left, anything they find lying around, gets kicked into place. Whole thing's up on blocks."

"We've little enough for ourselves."

"We'll work, help in every way we can. Build. Repair. Care for the sick and injured. We don't ask that a place be given us among you, we'll earn that twice over."

THE TRUE MEASURE OF a society comes down to how it treats its elderly, its children, the weakest in its group, Ahmed told us. This was at the end of a long afternoon he'd passed explaining governments to us, how they form tribally, to protect the group from outsiders, then, as they evolve, turn that motive inward, toward protecting the weaker among their own. The tear in the fabric, he said, is that in time the overseers come to believe that stability resides solely with them, such that holding their position becomes important above all else.

In that other world, Ahmed had been a journalist, a de facto historian, he said—as now he'd become our de facto teacher. One of many stories he told us was of his youthful journey into the swamps far down south, a truly fantastic land of alligators, new frontiersmen and swarms of insects so dense they blocked out the light of a noonday sun. We were enthralled.

Parents set to showing our newcomers around. How we lived, what we grew, edibles to be gathered from the land, trapping and dressing squirrel and rabbit.

Early on, Ahmed had taken to spending considerable time with Donse and me. Then, I wondered if this might be because he missed his own children. Later I came to understand that, with his having so much to learn about this new world in which he found himself, our uncomplicated take on things helped ease his passage, his way in.

Donse and I had been told about holidays. We never had or observed them, but the day the others arrived was close enough.

They came in an actual automobile, a gray one with splotches of reddish, clay-looking stuff smeared on here and there. We'd never smelled anything as awful as that thing, and it came in smoking like it was soon not to be. Bruiser, Ahmed called it. No shocks, he said, whatever those were. No shocks, bad tires, worse roadways—when there were roadways at all. The two who had come with Ahmed left and returned, six days later, with our new residents.

A dark, short-haired woman drove the car, with Ahmed's friends and two kids, one of them a boy around our age, inside. Justin. He and his younger sister, Joanna, looked nothing alike. Their mom, when she climbed out of the car, proved to be as tall as any of our male parents. There was something odd or stiff about how she moved, as though bone and muscle didn't fit together quite as they should.

Parents had cleared out one end of a supply shed for new arrivals. Two more had moved in with other parents to leave their shed open. Good thing too, since by late afternoon black fists of clouds began forming and by nightfall opened to let loose heavy rains.

By morning the village was a mess. Took us hours of shoveling mud, hauling tree limbs and shoring up all kind of slippage, to get it into anything resembling shape. You couldn't help but notice how the newcomers jumped right in, kids included, Justin and Joanna kind of watching out the side of their eyes to see what we were doing, doing the same, going along.

THEY HAD LIVED, JOANNA said, in a place called Holding. When people fled the cities, some, like the Parents, went far and embraced a new beginning, but most settled close to the towns and cities they'd left. In time these makeshift camps sprouted tents and temporary dwellings to become villages, then more substantial structures to become, themselves, small towns. Holding was one of those. There'd been a hospital of sorts there, and a school. Playgrounds where she and Justin met old friends and made new ones. People got together in groups to cook, talk and share food.

When we asked Ahmed about this, if it was all true, he said yes. When we asked why he and the others had left, he thought for a moment (one sensed words falling together in his mind) before telling us that it all had begun to feel too familiar, that they'd grown fearful the settlements were heading down the same path as before.

I was eight when Ahmed and the others joined us, eleven when Peacekeepers came in open-back trucks, with wooden cages built over the truck beds, to relocate us. From as early as we could remember, Parents had told us such might happen at any time. Freedom camps, these were called, initial steps in the new government's attempt to reunify a country shattered from a lack of common beliefs, to begin anew at the community level, and from those diverse communities rebuild the nation. We were given our own area within the sprawling grounds and allowed to remain together. Huts and upgraded lean-tos for residence, a common galley space with dugout pantry, communal tanks of water nearby.

Each camp held weekly council meetings. Why was I in attendance? I had no idea what was going on. But I remember those meetings—faces mostly, some passive, others awash with thought, as questions, formulations, proposals and objections made their way around the galley tables, Ahmed explaining to us afterward that one group insists the meetings, even the camps themselves, serve only to give an illusion of freedom, while another group bears down hard on responsibilities that have to be shared, the first shouting *Control*, the second *Freedom*, neither hearing the other.

There at the camp, in what might be thought of as graduations or as promotions, I moved from latrine caretaker to fetch-and-carry tech to supply-shed accountant to farmer, becoming a champion grower of squash and beans. The challenge, the expertise such as it was, lay in squeezing everything possible from whatever you had at hand. Nutrients, space, water. There's only so much of any one thing in the world, Ahmed would say, only so much, and no idea, no words, could create more of it.

Water. Manure. I hadn't come so far from that latrine job after all.

I HEAR HER IN the next room, tapping away at the keyboard. Her voice is low and arhythmic, like an actor trying out phrasing, pace, delivery. I've asked why she vocalizes as she types and she tells me that the words, and what she's writing about, never seem real or right to her unless she does so. When she was eight, she figured out how to type on her brother's creaky dinosaur of a computer. He'd been drafted. She'd think the words, say them, move fingers, and they'd appear on the page, out there in the world. It felt like a miracle.

Everything here is teeth, Sophia said. That long-past year, early spring, with blooms appearing on trees as though from nowhere, we were in a town called Ghetr, hunkered down in an abandoned building waiting for the go-code, surviving off the latest field muck. Nearly half the ration packages were defective. You learned to check carefully for bloating or leaked seams. Through what remained of windows we watched ragged patrols move haphazardly about the streets. Far right, near the edge of town and visibility, twice within the hour, armored vehicles cruised by.

"Teeth," she said again. "Drink the water, you get dysentery. Cut your hand on a doorway, four days later infection sets in. Meanwhile, bugs the size of your big toe and others so small you can't even see them are chewing at you, the heat's like a blade and the humidity's so bad that blue-green fungus sprouts on your skin. Every damn thing there is, is out to get you."

"Not to mention those well-outfitted gentlemen down there."

"It does appear we're seriously outnumbered."

"Good thing we have manifest destiny on our side."

"Now if only we had weapons that didn't jam, adequate ammunition and vests that actually worked, there'd be no limit to what we might do."

"Edible food too, since we're dreaming."

"Why not."

For all the vividness of physical memory (shadows slow on the wall, bodies sour, heat rising in visible waves outside) I can no longer recall what our goal was that day, or exactly who we were fighting, a recognized government or some faction pitched against same. I do remember this was Sophia's and my fifth incursion into what was officially neutral territory.

Such had been my passage out of camp into a

larger world and my introduction to the epic life of dissolving footwear, failed equipage, hunger, exhaustion, unhealing wounds and dysentery. Others at the camp had asked why. We're safe here, they said, as safe as can be had, anywhere. We're provided for, protected. Food, shelter, supplies, clothing. Why would you leave? Ahmed, when I told him of my decision, simply nodded. Days later, for reasons (by agencies?) unknown, Ahmed himself was gone.

Past the shattered windows, personnel came into sight and out again, as anonymous, as interchangeable, as ourselves. In one extended deploy, we had six different COs.

OF A MORNING SOME months ago, without prelude, I'd received a wave from her. As had become my habit, I was sitting in a café across from the temporary capitol with a second coffee and what I thought of as homework, vetting and signing off on the week's burden of requisition slips and POs. I'd just looked up to watch what seemed a fleet of delivery trucks stream down the street and considered for the first time how much labor and how many workers were intimately involved in getting this city fed. My screen blinked, and when I nodded, there it was. No visual, text only.

> Hope this finds you well, little soldier boy.
> A few days back I looked to see who was

currently running this shitshow and came across your name tucked away in a far corner like it was too shy for company or the big guns don't want to admit to it. I'd ask you to tell me it's not so, but apparently it is. Things must be even worse than I thought. No wars, though. That sounds good, even if it's not true. (Is it ever?)

While you've been spending your days making sure the government's supply of jockstraps is adequate and helping decide if a post office is necessary, I've been involved with security of another stripe. Not long after we left service, I wandered up into the Midwest, great portions of which have fractured into family-led communities. With no government protection forthcoming, many employ private militias fashioned from the spillover soldiers of our recent wars. Until last month, I worked for one of these families, before being curtly dismissed. And yes—it was something I said.

So now I'm back in the mainland of this grand nation, and what do I find? That you, you of all people, have a hand in running it.

> You know, each time, I thought the world I came back into after the war would be a different one. But there is no "after the war," is there? There's only recurrence, realignment, reloading.

No great surprise, then, when Sophia surfaced weeks later. Not that I'd expected it, but the moment she walked up to my table at the café, where I sat working not at requisitions this time but at the intricate fascinations of departmental budgeting, the thought *Well of course!* arrived with her.

Given the lack of available quarters in our hastily assembled capitol, with junior staff living in less junior's closets, I had little choice but to offer one of my luxurious two tiny rooms as temporary shelter. The few days became a week, as they will, then, when she happened on to work as an archivist, with no discussion from either of us, more or less permanent.

"They have an archive," she told me that evening. "An actual archive—can you imagine? The government's been around, what, a year?"

"A bit more."

"Not much. At first I thought the interviewer was saying they had a position for an anarchist."

"Ah . . . such disappointment."

"Well, I was qualified for that, at least. For this one, as near as I can tell, my qualification consists of being able to remember where I put things. I do have a desk."

"A good sign."

"And I have two dozen like me sitting butt to butt rounding up free-range data bits, slapping on spit to paste them together. I look right or left, front or back, that's what I see. And you can bet every last one of us is thinking, Here you go, future, here's to you!"

"On such responsibilities are lives built."

"This is what lives have come to? Cataloging our past?"

"I'm not sure they ever amounted to much else."

We got on well, Sophia minding the past and me doing what I could to keep the present afloat. By tacit agreement we never spoke of our days in service. Instead, she heard about my early life in the mountains and the camp, and I learned of hers at a religious colony initially sanctioned then, with that government's collapse, struck down by locals. Like locusts coming through, she said. They showed up, swarmed, and when they were done, so was everything we'd built. Most of us just left.

Work, the routine of it, and the rituals with which we bolstered ourselves—my tenures at the café, Sophia's volunteer stints at the women-and-children shelter—kept much at bay. But the past and its fraught memories were never far off, carts packed high with goods, waiting for the chance to show what they had.

Again I come back to questioning what I might hope to accomplish. What does a memoirist do other than say *This is how I came to be here*, then pretend for eighteen pages, 145 or 300 that he or she actually knows? Can all those pages amount to much more than asking the same questions, tapping at the same drums, over and again?

OUR GOVERNMENT LUMBERED ON, stable beyond and despite its crazy-quilt composition. From no particular motive or plan, more or less in the same manner as, bulwarked by ritual, we got through our days, Sophia and I fell into the habit of meeting with others midweek at one of the cafés near the capitol for lunch. The assemblage was ever changing, our conversation a mélange of office talk, domestic reportage and fanciful soundings.

"If there *were* ghosts, why would they appear?" Fil might ask, his hands raised, then opening—to release the ghost?

"Maybe to warn us?" Gayle suggests, and mimics looking about nervously. "And of what?"

"To attend to some unfinished business of their own."

"Or somehow to go on living, briefly, grayly, on the wash of *our* lives?"

It was there, at Café Lu, that the name Noel began entering Sophia's conversation. Over a period of weeks I learned that he grew up on one of the coasts, a small town, it would seem; his brother was a college teacher, himself a government aide. They had met, she and Noel, when he showed up at the archive, where no one ever showed up, seeking certain documents from the prior administration that proved to be, to their mutual astonishment, actually there. The two of them had searched together.

Are all stories love stories? I suspect they are, in much the same sense that all are ghost stories, tales of things lost, reverberations, emblems of longing.

Sophia and I were living then, having recently changed quarters, in two rooms above a bar and grill properly named Abyss, popularly known as The Hole. From either room we could see the capitol itself, the scatter of two-story buildings surrounding it and, behind these, the ragged skyline of what, following upon the last decade's ablutions, still passed for a city.

To one of the gatherings at Café Lu she brought the mysterious Blaze's latest novel. No one, even the publisher, it was said, knew who he was. The books themselves were mysteries, initially of a classic sort: murder, suspects, interrogations, clues, leads, resolution. Over time they began bending more toward social commentary and character portraiture, becoming ever leaner, ever less structured. Of late, with Blaze rumored to be in his eighties, the novels had come to deal exclusively with missing persons. I'd soon have reason to recall that conversation.

Noel and I were never to meet. Sophia became frequently away, often for the night, sometimes for days at a time, then one evening returned to ask me to have dinner with them the following day. Noel failed to meet us as planned. Angry, embarrassed and fearful in equal part (then, I did not understand the fearfulness), Sophia left and was absent from the apartment for days.

One night close to midnight, looking not at all good, she returned to tell me that Noel was missing.

"There's no sign he's been to his flat all week. Or as near as I can tell, to his offices—though no one will say much of anything."

I ushered her into the kitchenette. We went on talking as I made tea. "I know he's an aide, but what exactly does Noel do, who does he work for?"

"Well . . ." She came close, as though to help with the tea. Classic evasion. Then, fully aware what she was doing, stopped herself.

"When he spoke about work, it was generic. He'd shy away from questions. Buffer."

"So you thought—"

"I did."

We went back across the room. She settled onto one of the chairs.

"I tracked him down on the directory. Interesting

body language at the listed office when I asked to see him."

"I'd imagine."

"Sometimes you have to shake the jar, see what turns up."

So it was that an hour or so past midnight, violating curfew, I stood beside Sophia just inside a flat at city's edge. Getting in had required three tries at the lock.

"A bit spare, isn't it?" she said. "He had a regular flat near the capitol. This one, I didn't know about—till last night."

Spare it was. Single straight-backed chair, plain table by it, foldable cot. Stacked cups and plates on a waist-high shelf with tea, coffee, biscuits and the like. Battered micro-cooker and electric camp stove. A rack of electronic equipment. All of it neat, orderly.

"There's no sign of a personality," I said, "no footprint. One way or another, everything here's about efficiency."

I'd strayed over to the single window, which actually, with some undoing of latches and use of force, opened. Bird seed had been scattered on the sill—regularly, judging by grains left behind in frame and lower rail.

When had I last seen birds here in the city?

Sophia stood by the table across the room, holding a link she'd picked up. "Coded." She made several runs at the keys. "No."

"Doesn't matter. There's nothing here. It's an empty box."

She agreed, and we went back out onto the street, staying close in against buildings, skirting what lights or lit areas we encountered. No one else on the streets, of course, after curfew. Theoretically.

"Sorry to bring you out for naught," she said. "I don't know what I had in mind that I'd find here."

She glanced over a couple of times when we made sudden turns, finally said, "We're being followed."

"Observed, anyway. Twice I've caught glints of moonlight off what has to be a drone. Could be routine, of course."

"Why would they track us?"

"Presumably they have some interest in what we're doing."

"Then why hold back? We're past curfew, they don't need further cause."

"Maybe it's not us they're after. Maybe it's one hand not knowing what the other hand's doing. Or maybe it's not the government at all."

THEY'D PAID VISITS TO my office as well. Habits of suspicion are hard to lose, habits I'd grown up with, so I'd installed catchkills—illegal, all but impossible to detect, effective—on my worklines. Early that morning, not long after Sophia's and my observed jaunt, someone had been carefully pacing the edges of them.

Meanwhile, ever the blundering oblivious brute, life went on. In an attempt to get Sophia's mind, both our minds, off Noel, I insisted on taking her out for dinner at Fatoul's and, afterward, a light comedy at Last Breath Theater. The play was indeed bright and well done, clipping along at any easy pace, but neither of us could sink into it though we gave it our best, laughing along with those around us, exchanging participatory glances at the witty parts.

By the time the theater let out, afternoon's clouds had ripened to an eager rain that came in bursts, dumping water by the bucketful, pulling back only to return full force. Shallow waves ran along the train platform beneath the canopy.

Home, we sloshed our way across the floors, wrung out sopping clothes as best we could and hung them in the bathroom. Went to bed but it wouldn't take. We passed the night telling stories from old lives.

Sophia's father had been a policeman, though they were called constables, in the midsize town where she lived as an older child. This was after her time in the religious colony, during the first Secession Wars; he took the job for its military deferment. As she grew up, the house was stuffed full of what he called liberated materials, links and other electronics in the living room, cases of scarce foodstuff in bedroom and kitchen, medical supplies of every sort, small appliances, tools—even weapons, she now assumed.

When she was fifteen, he disappeared. The next day, men showed up, uniformless but well-armed. Three took positions around the house, two came inside. They didn't identify themselves, only asked again and again where her father was. They stayed for hours, searched repeatedly through the house and finally left. To this day she didn't know who they were. And as far as she knew, no one ever saw or heard from her father again.

Not all that uncommon at the time, of course, she said. There were hundreds of such disappearances. Soldiers, rival politicians, intellectuals and teachers, journalists.

I told her of my friend Isaac, who was indeed a journalist though even for that profession something of a rogue, and who had disappeared with as many as a thousand others in a takeover of what was then the capitol. Later battles than those when Sophia was young, these with their own particular grand visions behind them, but it all finally came down to much the same.

For my part, I spoke as I rarely had of my family, of their concern at the way things were heading when we fled the city, back before our mountain life, before the Peacemakers and the camps.

"Did they actually believe they could leave all that behind?" Sophia asked of our time in the mountains.

"It was more like finding distance. Space to breathe. Did they believe it would last? I don't think so. Definitely they didn't think it was some edenesque childhood we were to remember for the rest of our lives. But maybe we took something of that distance, the breathing space, away with us."

I told her about Ahmed from the camps as well. Ahmed's last story before he vanished was about the Cracow bugler. At the turn of each hour, day or night, he said, even now, a bugler mounts 272 steps to the highest point of St. Mary's Basilica and, from a small room there, sounds the call, first in the direction of the Royal Castle, then toward market square, next to the Florian Gate and finally toward the headquarters of the fire brigade entrusted with stewardship of the tradition. The call is the *hejnał mariacki* and has rung out over Poland since the 1200s. The call is each time cut off abruptly, in remembrance of the bugler in 1241 who, sounding the alarm for invading Mongol forces and thereby saving the city, was shot in the neck by a Mongol's arrow.

Now *that*, Ahmed said, is history.

And if I had said, as I would now, that much of the bugler story was doubtless made up, Ahmed would have replied that this didn't matter. That history is seldom other than the stories we decide to tell ourselves, and we are little other than those stories, those decisions.

THAT MORNING AT WORK, office managers and

techs showed up to execute an audit of all links. There was reason, they said, to suspect an encysted virus. Six links wound up getting carted away for further testing, mine included. Daft from lack of sleep, I looked on half comprehending. The link came back within the hour. They must have found the illegal catchkills, and must have removed them, but nothing was said. Without a word the tech replaced it on my desk and backed away.

The remainder of the day passed uneventfully. That evening during heavy traffic hours I made a visit to an unkempt bodega across town, was ushered into the back and emerged with an obscenely expensive and fulsomely illegal link. In constant hopscotch mode, piggybacking off other links far and near, this would get me as close to untraceable and untrackable as it was possible to be. In my audits a year before, I'd come upon certain requisitions and miscellaneous budgetary items that had something of a smell about them and, breaking out old skills, followed the trail of those disbursements to the outlaw links. At the time I never imagined that any need of such links would arise, but I kept their source (another old habit) in mind.

There had to be traces of Noel at his nominal workplace, a spoor, leavings. Sidetracks. For reasons as unclear to me as they were unshakeable, though sympathetic to Sophia, I wasn't quite where she was with Noel's disappearance. Questions mitose. You have the first one, it splits into two, each one carrying the same basic stuff as the first.

Chances that the old nest remained active were slim as sticks, but I thumbed the link up and, dredging memory, entered lines of code laden with dips, dodges and redirects. Fourteen heartbeats passed before the cursor appeared. I imagined the link as a hand scrabbling at the tabletop, reaching out, groping for connection.

I entered my old ID.

A longer delay this time. Then what amounted to an oversized question mark.

I entered a secondary ID.

Communication on the nest had always been in a hybrid code that owed as much to pictograms and ASL as to traditional written language. What came up on the screen wasn't the same as that I was familiar with, but it was close enough, comprehensible the way a dialect can be to those speaking the origin language.

My correspondent at the other end expressed surprise.

That I'm in touch or that I'm alive, I asked, using the code for the first time in many years.

With that, and a respondent digital laugh, we set to negotiation. The nest having been founded by and maintained by anarchists, there was no chain to work my way up, but patience and serial handoffs at length gained assurance that Cyl, if he so wished, would be in touch. Cyl was a legend for staying free of courts and correctional facilities for half a century through multiple governments; before that, simply for his unholy skills. Words like *genius, wizard* or *linemaster* often came up at mention of him, as did *treason, criminal* or *treachery.* There seemed no code, network, firewall, deep fix or encryption he couldn't storm.

He was online with me within the hour. I was watching coverage of protestors bodily blocking traffic in the area around the capitol, bringing trains and sub to a stop, as I recalled stories—and memories—of how such had been dealt with in years past. Crawlers had taken over the bottom of the screen:

> See Only the News YOU Want
> News That Matters to YOU

A recog for the old nest flashed for half a second before the entire screen went blank. I hit reset, functions and keys indiscriminately. Nothing. Then, without prompts or preamble, everything was back.

"Speak freely. Your link's rebuilt."

Voice only. The screen showed a small cottage, blue sky above, path winding downhill to a lake or bay.

"That's impossible."

"Of course it is. Ask anyone."

"And the link was safe already."

"Links are send-receive units, rooms with information as furniture. The furniture can be moved around. New shelves, new chairs. Rugs. Storage."

"I doubt that."

"Doubt is a good thing, hold on to it. But then, you always have."

"You know who I am."

"Your contributions are well remembered. Whatever those may or may not have to do with this backdoor visit and your current occupation."

I filled him in on Noel's relationship with Sophie and her concern at his abrupt disappearance, the dead end we'd reached making inquiries at his supposed workplace both in person and by online rain-dancing, the audit of links at my own office. Leaving out my suspicions.

"No mention made of your catchkills," Cyl said. "Interesting. Let me swim upstream, see what's there."

News came back onscreen, complete with new crawlers, as I waited. Last night and this morning, insurrectionists—the term was used in each sentence that dropped from the announcer's lips—had made their appearance known, striking at a number of intensely monitored government sites. The sites, which included federal offices, government data banks, police and military records, had not been actively breached, but at each site the insurrectionists had left behind the cartoon logo of a huge bare foot lodged in a door.

Attacks from protestors and parapoliticals occurred almost daily. They were seldom news. The scope and extent of these strikes was shocking, though, as was the fact that knowledge of the incursions was so freely being released to the public.

Minutes later, the screen returned to cottage, sky and water. Cyl was back.

"There's what you'd expect on top. Birthplace, schools, employment, residences, accounts. Deeper, and it starts thinning out."

"Potemkin village? All appearance?"

"Either that or someone's been at the data, scouring it."

"Why would they do that?"

"They. He. Who knows? Rewrite or removal. He have reason to disappear? Someone need to have him be missing?"

I remember sitting there with what Cyl said rolling about in my head, they or he, he have reason, someone need him not be around, thinking about the strafing runs at my office link, the purported virus, my catchkills, Noel's lack of footprint or face, the drone that tracked Sophia and me.

I realized I hadn't responded to Cyl when he spoke up again: "What made you suspicious?"

Again, moments went by before I answered.

"Years ago, first time in cities, I had this friend, Jorge. He'd been adopted and when he was a kid, his parents owned a deli. He used to swear to me that they had this one cheese that came in huge wheels and had holes like Swiss. At night, he said, when no one was around and it got dark, cockroaches poked their heads from the holes, looked around and scampered out."

Both of us were quiet.

"Governments are like that cheese," I said.

"Always. And still are: the whole time I was upstream just now, I had linemen banging away at me. Government, anarchists, protestors . . . No way to know."

"I haven't put you in danger, have I?"

"Where I live. By the time they bite down, I'm somewhere else. Most jumpers aren't all that shiny. See this, punch in that. I'll stay on the circuits, see what else turns up."

AT WORK, NOTHING MORE came of the audits and supposed concern over encysted viruses. Out in the world, that week brought selective shutdowns of solar panels, wind turbines and sea-ketches, presumably by protestors, then power losses and brownouts the government insisted must not be construed as response to, or in any way related to, the shutdowns.

Next, the city's garbage reclamation centers got picketed complete with lie-ins, bringing two almost to a full stop. Protestors, the majority of them students, were arrested, detained for documentation and released.

Cyl's sign off, *I'll stay on the circuits, see what else turns up*, lodged in my mind even then as a fair summary of our lives.

These pages keep leaning into the wind, feigning by turns, it would seem, to become post-apocalypse tale, bildungsroman, espionage thriller, love story, even mawkish political satire. In the end, they may prove little more than their writer figuratively throwing up his hands.

Luckily, whatever it is, this isn't fiction. I'm not required to offer up a sympathetic character. Nor am I bound to represent events in chronological order or, for that matter, any order at all. In short, this impression of what has gone by doesn't have to make sense. Most of it never did at the time.

All those songs and stories beginning "There was a time when everything was fine"? This isn't one of those.

Toward the end of that month, midweek, Sophia didn't show up at the apartment after work, and when later on I waved the archives, I got only a billboard asking me to please call again during hours. Messages to Sophia's personal link went unanswered. Attempts the next morning to her workplace fared no better. She was out of office, I was kindly informed, and nothing more. Solemn and silent, two days went by, then three.

That was the day insurgents shut down pretty much everything and surrounded the Capitol in self-constructed armored cars, taking control of the city, its immediate surround and every citizen thereof.

HOW IT WAS THAT under constant and thoroughgoing surveillance those cars and such revolutionaries came to be, remains unanswered, as does the question of why military, militia, police and Peacekeepers failed to intervene and challenge this takeover.

The web went dark. Eventually, personal links came back, but all nests stayed dormant. Cameras and sniffers as well were said to have gone nonfunctional—rumor further holding that their nerve centers had been destroyed by the insurgents. By the new government.

From my rooms and the building's rooftop I watched the come-and-go of groups both orderly and unkempt around the Capitol, looked down into those milling in the streets, foundered as they were by sudden loss of occupation and of the commonplace. Many strayed for food and drink into The Hole on my building's ground floor.

I had tried to communicate. Everything at the Capitol appeared to be shut down. Reports began to arrive of break-ins all about the city, lootings, fires set, riots, unfocused violence. Then of mass arrests. Much of this, of course, was false, but it became clear that former members of the government were in fact being searched out and detained. Such rumors develop a life of their own and grow quickly. Soon, officials were said to have been taken to this place or that. Inquisitions were underway. The city was undone.

It had been undone many times before. History stutters, but eventually gets the word out. Images of that time persist; many of you have seen them, the deserted buildings, abandoned streets. The stillness. You well may have wondered, like myself even now, just what you are bringing to the experience of those images, to your understanding of them. What memories, what longing, what imagining.

They did come for me early one afternoon, four remarkably polite, deferential young men. The scene itself was familiar enough, strangers showing up (though this time not unexpectedly) to take me some place else.

I was escorted to a well-lit central facility, questioned amiably by an interlocutor who gave the impression of feeling as out of place in the surroundings as did I, and released by day's end. The greater part of their questions, often indirectly, had to do with Sophia.

Months later, agape with wonder and bloated with questions ever to go unanswered, I would see her and (I assume) the man she knew as Noel onlink, speaking for the new government.

I LEFT THE CITY not long after. It had remained for a time in lockdown, and once restrictions passed, I gathered up those few things that might serve for survival and departed. Recalling Ahmed's tales of swamps, alligators and solitude, especially that last, I aimed south, into mile upon mile of disintegrating roadways, towns in thrall to new wilderness, ragged camps, makeshift colonies. Notions of time and of distance lost relevance. One moved and kept moving, that was the whole of it. Sometimes, both among fellow travelers and in settlements, I encountered kindness, including offers of food and travel advice, even shelter; other times, hostility and aversion. I ate mushrooms, nuts and berries such as I could find, upon occasion was able to scavenge canned or preserved foods from abandoned houses, stores and cabins.

I really have no firm notion of where I went to ground, which is to say, where I am. Well along, perhaps, in what was once Mississippi, possibly Texas or Louisiana swampland, in a small cabin, maybe once a fishing cabin, maybe once a home to generations of family, on a bay tucked away in dense forests of oak, pine and cypress.

So was it that I found myself heir to two usable pans, an iron skillet, three woebegone chairs, a pallet with pretense to being a bed, a table with two legs lower than the other two and none of the four at level, protective shields of dirt and plant life on every surface and a menagerie of spiders and lizards watched over by a huge frog.

Such had become my civilization. My nation of one.

Definitely I cannot recommend relearning how to clean and cook fish, birds and the occasional squirrel by trial and error, or to learn in that manner what plants are edible. Over months the learning got done, but at considerable cost and not without days of near-mortal illness and of fear. A distinct advantage, though, lay in the fact that just about anything one stuck in the ground grew (or so it seemed) overnight. Anyone who could live off algae and fungi would be set for life.

That was scarcely the worst, however.

Often in my life I'd been afraid, terrified even, beginning as a child when Peacekeepers came to take us to the camps, but never more so than when, some months into my time on the bay, foraging in the woods and thankfully not too far in, I lost my footing near an unseen ravine, tumbled down it and broke my lower left leg, a compound fracture.

Dragging myself about, I was able to fashion a splint of sorts from branches found aground and vines torn away from root systems. A lengthy rest did little by way of recovery, but I then managed to pull myself back to the clearing, a passage that must have taken hours. There I contrived a sling-and-noose that, anchored, let me reset the bone as well as possible given circumstance, limitations and pain. Using wood I'd previously split and set aside for fires, around the leg from hip down I constructed what was essentially a cast, fitting it close to stabilize and immobilize the leg while still allowing for swelling. Above the rupture itself I left a window. Infection was a deadly nightmare of its own, and all but inevitable in the situation.

I worked hourly to keep the wound clean, staggering and stumping and mostly hopping about with a rude crutch, using gallons of the bay's water, applying moss and matted spider webs to the site as dressing. In the cabin I had stocks of garlic, sage and honey, all of them, I knew, natural antibiotics.

This experience brought to the foreground knowledge I'd carried with me unvoiced to what increasingly I thought of as my settlement: The recognition that our lives, individually, communally, socially, are never linear but are, instead, forever messy and jumbled—not a single story but a collection of them, anthologies of our lifelong grappling for safe ground.

It also gave cause and time to reflect upon society's

ever-present predictors of cataclysm, on all prophets of doom with their fixation, their excitement, about the end. How the end when it came would mean they were right, terminally right. How there could be no rejoinder, no challenge, no further question.

The fracture healed to allow something like normal usage in what was probably (no calendars here, of course) four months. By six I felt the worst danger was done with. Crutches gave way to a sturdy cane, the wooden cast my leg had lived in got moved along, piece by piece, to other use. I'd somehow escaped not only serious blood loss and clots but also, wonder of wonders, severe infection.

Not long after, as I hobbled about, my first visitor arrived.

He was in poor shape initially, but decent nourishment and rest soon had him up and about, pitching in alongside me as I worked to recoup all I'd let slide while incapacitated.

That first day he told me his name was Parel—after a musician popular when his mother was young, he said—and not much else. Late twenties, lanky, with one of those faces that seem forever intent yet show no emotion. Beautiful amber eyes. He explained, apologetically, that most of his life had been spent moving from place to place, never alighting, and because of this he could tell me little, bring no practicable news, of the world beyond. I told him

I'd come to realize that I had no need of such. He spoke in an odd patois, one perfectly understandable but slippery and askew, vocabulary and usage (I assumed at the time) knocked together from whatever he happened to hear as he moved about. Later he confirmed this impression. He'd been brought up, he said, by parents fallen ill with a debilitating and deadly illness, one that went from person to person in his village and well beyond, and after they died, having taught him only basic speech, at age nine he'd gone away from there and out into the world alone.

After Parel, others came, but none stayed. Some bore news and rumor: outbreaks of typhus and smallpox in the Western Alliances; a workers' coup in Old Virginia; parts of the upper western seaboard closed down completely, guarded by militia.

I'm thrown back onto memories of how we believed, each time, that we would change the world—that the betterments our protests, political group or government sought were inevitable. Now I wonder if we're not fatally paralyzed, as a society, as a nation, even as a species, by habit and our presumptions. The self-narratives by which we chart our course over time harden and set to the point they're believed unassailable. Whatever threat befalls, be that threat military, financial, defiance from within, weakness or disease, it challenges the narrative, suggesting the narrative is false—and the narrative has to be supported at any cost.

Sitting here waiting for my owls to return, knowing they won't, here at the edge of what was once a country and of just about everything else (time as well, some might say), it comes to seem that for the whole of history every society, every nation, has found itself set blindly toward returning to some imagined prior form—innocence, equity, godliness—that never in fact existed.

The owls, I watched from birth. Their parents had settled into a live oak at woods' edge not far from the cabin. Barred owls, who love the swampland and these ancient forests, who typically don't migrate or move about much at all but pass their eight years or so of life in the same location. Eight or ten days after I suspected hatching, I saw young in the nest; a month later, quite awkwardly at first, they were learning to fly, and after another week of circling back to the nest, they were gone.

This year (to the best of my reckoning, now that time has gone fluid, or fictional) I am forty-two.

One final memory, following which I'll put an end to this scribbling and to my attempt at nudging words into some semblance of meaning or, if not meaning, then at least honest description.

A political huddle, among the last I recall. Our chair, for some reason speaking of either the Romantic or Modern age, remarked, "There was a time, you know, when we believed we might catch a glimpse of the actual world in the visions of madmen." To which another participant added, "Then we came to believe the same of politicians," and yet another, "Such is the world's history."

Asked about the dawn of civilization in an interview, anthropologist Margaret Mead told of shelters in which skeletons with healed leg fractures were found, indicating that others in the group had taken care of those injured and unable to care for themselves until the fractures healed. *That*, she said, was the beginning of civilization.

The naked spirit should have sanctuary, novelist Ann Petry wrote. This is mine.

Sanctuaries are also shores, and from time to time (that word again, *time*, its snout pokes at everything) others of the shipwrecked find their way here. One day, I have no doubt, I'll head back out to sea myself: a voyage, an adventure, a leaving, a return. But for now the waters by the cabin are calm, and though my owls are gone, among the birch, maple, oak and cypress festooned with Spanish moss, young birds sing.

ALLOTMENTS

When we saw the wounds of our country
appear on our skins,
we believed each word of the healers.

—Faiz Ahmed Faiz

Every few weeks the older folks gather on the square to tell their stories.

For them, Paolo says, it was a big thrill. They weren't supposed to go into the city, even near it, but they always found ways. Out for a hike, they'd tell parents—and they'd be in the city. Off to Theo's, a bunch of them were getting together to play—the city again. They'd make their way through, past and over the wreckage, go into buildings it's a wonder didn't collapse on them, paw through what was left, find things. Half the time they didn't even know what the things were. Tobie, went by T, picked up what they found out later was a flute. None of them had ever seen anyone play instruments or heard much by way of music. And T couldn't play it, but did. All the time. Got so they'd run when he showed up with the thing. T kept saying there weren't enough notes on it, that he was hearing stuff in his head that couldn't be played on what he called *the pipe*, so one day he got a punch drill and added some new holes. That's how it got started. Not long after, they were all trying to play. Making their own instruments. Making up how to play them as they went along.

Prima tells this one.

When she was five or six months old, her parents put her, in the shopping basket they used as a carrier, under the table at a café. Cafés had just begun reopening after the blackouts. They'd gone into one, though reluctantly and with misgivings, and placed her beneath the table. Before they even ordered, the bomb went off. Her parents were killed in the blast. She has been deaf from that day. From time to time, even now, she says, she tries to imagine, as novelists and actors might imagine themselves into her silent world, what it would be like to live in a world of sound.

We all have our stories here.

I was born in the year of their lord 23. The last revolution, they claimed it to be, that which had waited in the wings for decades and now was to have its time. Revolutions comprise definitive, extreme change; this one seemed more in line with clambering back to how things once were, or how they were imagined. Extremes, however, proved to be of great use in the push and rush to get there.

My parents were on the road, scampering from their tiny failed nation to a freehold just across the border, when my mother went into labor. Things had tightened down everywhere, and my parents believed this would be their last chance to get out. Guards at the checkpoint carried her into their tent, where, within the hour, she delivered. We spent a number of days in the home of one of the guards, a woman named Mirela who cared for us there, then, once recovered, were escorted across. My father was detained. Mother was never again to see him.

Nowadays I look at images of shallow, untraveled country roads and wonder how closely they resemble those my parents traveled. I wonder, too, what motive or reason the guards, especially Mirela, might have had to offer such kindness to Mother and myself while detaining my father. So much wondering, once you start. The past is forever murky water, I suppose: The more you stir at it, the murkier it becomes. History's never neat script, always a scrawl.

In what was for me home and for my mother eternally another country, I grew up not on children's books but on stories of Emma Goldman, Salvador Allende and Antonio Gramsci from the grand uncle with whom we came to live, a very old man by then, historian by profession. Never once did he offer stories of princes, frogs, magic or military grandness. Instead he told me of bodies piled four to six feet deep at town's edge, of fires that smoldered and never seem to go out, the ever present buzz of flies carpeting the bodies, of the smells. "The course of our lives isn't a given," he said, "it has to be taken—created." Many years later, a soldier fighting beside me, like myself a refugee from the south, told me how he and his fellows got jackbooted to clear bodies, hauling them from homes and yards and streets, stacking them like cordwood where directed, fully expecting to be shot themselves once they were done.

By way of my uncle I came to believe that many of the frames upon which we hang our lives—utopias, dystopias, moral tales, revenge stories, religious rites, tame mystery stories—are bent toward tamping down mankind's aggressive, bloody nature. When Thomas More insists that radical change in social governance will change human nature, we have to ask how any such transition to a better society can arise from a corrupt one, and we have to wonder if another Thomas, Thomas Hobbes, isn't more on point: That for any true change to take place, human nature itself must be radically modified.

Age six, of course, I knew and thought none of this, knew only that missiles often fell as days took hold, that explosions broke night's back, that sometimes we went for days and for weeks without power, without fresh water. When I asked who was doing this to us, my uncle would say, "The very regions from which we sprouted."

By the time I was ten, the wars were over, or had turned their faces elsewhere, and days passed at a steady pitch. The balance now had tipped to rethinking, my uncle said, to revisionism, realignments. Within the year, he lay dying. Our last conversation included that discussion of More and Hobbes. At the time it didn't occur to me that this was in any way odd. I assumed that all families in their private time together spoke in such manner and of such. My uncle that day told me again about Eugene Debs in prison for protesting war, how other political prisoners looked upon the criminals among them as a group apart while Debs understood that they and his fellow socialists were casualties of the same social machinery—to his mind, capitalist greed.

I remember, back then, my friend Edmond telling this story.

His mother died of cholera during the July Offensive. Edmond recalled how he sat at her bedside, how others joined her, that day at her bedside beside him, later in death, so that no one remained of his family. They all died, he said, of too much government. To which my mother, seldom moved to comment upon another's beliefs, responded: Or of too little.

WHEREAS THE NATION MY parents fled had been little more than a loose collective of old city-states, my new homeland sprawled to the sea on the far west and, easterly, abutted the borders of a host of independent yet allied nations. Our heady stew of diverse towns, settlements and people called itself simply The Commonwealth. Officials were volunteers vetted by the populace for two- or four-year terms, the word *vote* carefully avoided, the terms inextensible. Basic housing, employment, education, health care and family support were provided by the government.

Eight years after my uncle's death I entered into the voluntary service that would qualify me for higher education at university, *voluntary* in this case coming down to a choice between civil militia or national. Choosing the former, after three months of intensive training I spent the better part of as many years addressing domestic disputes, monitoring protests, helping investigate minor insurgencies and periodically providing guard details for government officials or official gatherings.

To this day I have no firm idea which might be preferable, too much government or too little, or even if the question itself makes sense. But I came to believe that government's prime obligation has to be to the safety and care of its citizens, especially those lacking position or influence, that this is the very foundation of society and that any government whose efforts swerve toward gaining or retaining power has abandoned its reason for being. With the years I've come to wonder, further, to what degree *all* our fine high ideas of government may be little more than comforting fictions.

At university, misguidedly but with the best of intentions, I started off studying law, then side-stepped to medicine, where I met Rain. Twenty or so years older than myself, Rain had served with the Free Marines, under their aegis traveling widely about the world. An astonishingly quick study, he knew portions of many languages. And he was a reader—from having lots of time aboard ship with not all that much to do, he said. Talking with him I learned of lives and cultures quite divergent from those I saw about me.

Founder's Hall 3 was a confusing mix of workers, students and minor government officials, two to a room, each of us with our very own pallet bed, with space for a couple of chairs and a table or desk, narrow closets and sufficient open floor left in the middle for us to step past one another. These dorms reared up, like the anthills they were, all over that part of the city at the time.

From medical school and an accelerated internship, by mandate I returned to public service, assigned, along with Rain and three others from our class, to an immigrant's camp near the eastern border. In theory a screening and holding facility, in practice it became—as officials wrung their hands and towns everywhere struggled to feed, house and care for current residents—a destination. Immigrants came and stayed. Many were ill. Many more would be, especially as winter came on. We were kept busy.

Greatly taken at the time with his readings in ancient history, Rain one morning announced, "It's as though we're heading back to civilization's beginnings." Paolo, fervid for the supposed grand perfections swirling about us, countered with, "No, we stand now at the very *cusp* of history." Mali: "Untethered from your own past, are you, then?" While Marta chimed in with words from an old poet who, she said, had seen this all before: "History licked the corners of its bloody mouth."

There were few moments allowing the leisure of such philosophy, however, always wounds to clean and stitch, minor surgeries, births, inoculations, infections, bones to set, dying souls to comfort as we could, the number of immigrants, the severity of their damage, ever increasing.

THEY CAME, OF COURSE, at night. Commandos,

I'm sure they believed themselves to be, a strike team, surgical in their own way. Cut through the fray of outlying guards, found and excised us.

The first leg of the journey was in the stale, stinking remains of an ancient delivery van, packed in there tight with no idea why we'd been taken or what danger we might be in, looking into the faces of our abductors, which seemed not so much fierce as bone tired and half ill.

It was not long before we turned off anything resembling a road, into woods to judge by our lurching, fitful progress, heads slamming against the roof, tree limbs and foliage raking at the van and clawing beneath, finally onto more level yet still rough ground. *Press gang, we'd have been called back in nautical days*, Rain remarked as we puzzled among ourselves as to what purpose or end we'd been taken.

Delivered were we at great length to their lair, doors swinging open on an abandoned village that might once have harbored thirty people, since moved into and overwritten by our captors. Tents of various sizes stood about. Many of both these and the original tumbledown cabins had acquired lean-tos. We were directed to a latrine past the first line of elms. *Most definitely we're well into the east countries*, Rain said as we returned to be fed a rich fish stew with bread, jugs of water set by us. Only then, as we ate, was our presence, our abduction, explained.

The speaker was a stump of a man with weather-creased skin like pale bark and bright green eyes. Moshe. None of the group wore uniforms, just workman's clothes in neutral colors that blended into the woodland surround.

We hardly knew what to expect: bits of the manifesto for some obscure people's revolutionary force, edicts from a cobbled-up army, appeals to the common good, unadulterated threats. By this time we'd heard all of that and much more elsewhere. What we got was a request—impolite, considering the circumstances, yes, and brash, but still a request—for help.

The battles in the east countries were far different and far worse than we had been told, Moshe said. Ravaged by civil war as much as by their battles against neighboring regions, the east countries, one and all, stood broken and bleeding. Legion upon legion of the wounded and dying lay about, dozens of civilians for every soldier, and but a handful of physicians to care for them, virtually none outside major settlements.

"So you took it in mind to forcibly import some," Rain said.

"You three. Others, we left. You've many in your land, yes?"

Rain nodded.

"Come with us, see for yourselves what I can but poorly describe. Remain with us, help us, until this savagery ends—"

"Savagery has an end?" Rain said.

"No. But often it looks in another direction."

"Yes."

"And that may be all we can hope for, all we can ask. That, and your help, now, for this moment. If after witnessing our need you elect not to stay, we'll see that you return safely to your homeland."

Everything in Moshe's address to us was respectful, spoken with great conviction and almost certainly untrue. Even then we knew that. But we went with Moshe and his adjutant Huy to a settlement further into the region, and we saw. Building after building filled with people on makeshift cots and pallets, maimed, eviscerated, severely burned, suffering dysentery, cholera, galloping infections. Paucity and utter lack of meds, splints, instruments, stitching, blood, bandaging, tubing, normal saline. Tubs of water used, chemically treated, then used again when no more was available. Dozen after dozen of the elderly and of children, those who have so few defenses, and of soldiers looking not much more than children themselves.

Mali chose to leave, while Rain and I stayed. To this day I've no idea what became of Mali, whether or not he made it back to the immigrant camp as promised, though I have my suspicions.

"HOW MANY DOES THIS make?" Huy asked. Looking down.

"We hadn't started counting till now. Better than twenty's my guess."

Bennie's flesh was liquefying in small, glistening patches, tide pools awash with particles, debris. A systemic infection we'd not seen before, nor did we possess resources to identify it.

We had set to work immediately, Rain and myself. The settlement was one of a number set back well behind the lines, tucked away in sheltered woodlands, wounded and ill brought in from all about. We were deep into broken bones, burns, open wounds, missing parts and infections, salvage work of the most grueling sort, when a singular grouping began to show up: reduced body temp, swelling of extremities, puffy joints, weeping from soft tissue, open mouth sores; then the patches, skin and flesh sloughing away, filling with bloody exudate. Viral, opportunistic, fast to take hold and as nasty as nasty gets. Nothing in our modest stash of antibiotics had much discernible effect. We could do little more than work to keep the sloughed areas clean and offer what palliatives and limited pain relief we had available.

Scoop, we began calling it. Starting up three weeks back, it had galloped its course so rapidly that fully a third of those in our care now showed signs.

Bennie was twelve, father killed by troops who passed through his town, mother dead not long after of what sounded to be internal bleeding. Bennie had gathered up his eight-year-old sister and a six-year-old orphaned neighbor and guided them in what he hoped was the right direction, away from active battle. They fed on insects and leaves from plants, eventually came across a group of refugees from whom Bennie pled help. Shortly the refugees, in turn, were come upon by a squad of Moshe's troops, the healthier among the refugees relocated, the rest brought here for treatment.

They all had stories.

Huy, for his part, was just then returning from a search for supplies, going into derelict towns to rummage through grocery and dry goods stores, pharmacies, aid centers and medical offices in hope of finding salvageable wound dressing, ointments, salve, splints or braces, supplements, meds. Under cover of night he'd even made the journey back to our old immigrant camp. Evidence of multiple raids, he told us. Not many people around, and them most likely squatters from the look of it. Place not much more than a shell now, he said. But he'd brought back a small cache of antibiotics and topical anesthetics, plus bags of normal saline. Elsewhere he'd unearthed boxes of cheesecloth that could serve as bandaging and of sewing thread that would do for stitches.

"Think a lot of this young man," he said, standing there by Bennie's cot.

"We all do."

"I'd best go fill Moshe in on all this."

"Of course."

Peace, it's been said, is the time it takes to reload. And what we never seem able to learn is that, following war, things don't go back to what they were before, they stay worse.

Just as the scoop got worse, day by day, hour by hour. Within weeks well over half those in our care were infected. We were skip-stepping from one failing body to the next, losing ground rapidly, when the settlement itself came under attack. Granted that red crosses, red crescents and such had been for different wars, different times, but still, the attack made no sense. Beyond refuge and medical care (lacking as the latter might be) there was nothing of warring interest in the settlement. No active soldiery, no militia, no storage of equipment or arms, certainly no excess food or other materials of value for the taking.

Because we were there?

It seemed they simply appeared among us. We looked up from our tasks and met eyes with them. In ragged formation, familiar uniforms. *Friendlies,* Rain said. *They're ours.* Forces we knew from the immigrant camp, our own, in The Commonwealth. *Best not to mention that.* We were all, everyone who was mobile, herded into two buildings under guards. Those who couldn't move or be moved got left where they were, unminded.

Huy and his small band in their workingman's clothes had disappeared as imperceptibly as the uniforms had arrived. And that very night, as the uniforms themselves fell under attack, Huy and his men slipping back into the settlement and upon them with the force of a sudden storm, Rain and I decided, in the confusion and disarray, to run. I told myself then that fleeing wasn't simple cowardice but came of some deep instinct for survival—one of many lies upon which my life floated at the time.

But what I carried away from the stories I heard in the settlement, like those of my uncle, have stayed with me. That war is always presented as a clash of grand ideas. That the true measure of war lies in the disasters that slough off onto everyday lives. That should you want to know something of any nation's soul, don't go to judges, administrators or interpreters, but to those in the greatest need, the overlooked, the ones who don't matter. Go and ask them.

FREE WE WERE, WITH absolutely no idea *where* we were. We hadn't a clue which way we should head. Farther into the eastern territories? Or back, toward the homeland whose soldiers had just precipitated our flight? How long a journey might the latter be, on foot and fatigued, with no water, no food? Nor could we envision what might await us in either direction.

We'd been too long away from civilization. We knew nothing of what west *or* east looked like now, or how battles among regions fared or at what level.

We walked to the point we could scarcely drag ourselves farther, fortuitously within sight of a small town, rallying strength and resolve sufficient to get there before collapsing. Whether in our thoughts we were entering the town to surrender, to beg alms or cry mercy, or to request asylum, quite honestly I can't recall. Rain later said that mostly what we were doing was trying very hard not to die.

The town was named Trace—after Benjamin Trace, its founder, we were later informed. He'd come up from the far south over forty years ago, bringing with him a large family and a genius for encouraging even reluctant soils to yield crops. At one time Trace had provided food for much of the region. With ongoing war, damage to the land and increasing isolation, nowadays the town could support its own needs but little more. They continued to do what they could by way of helping those neighbors close by.

Our orientation to the town came from Suze Warren, "mayor by default, more or less," she said, "no authority, no portfolio, only expectations." Barely out of her teens, she radiated quiet calm and confidence such as made it easy to envision her stepping into the role.

Once she'd told us the town's story, we shared ours

with her, told her about the raid on the settlement, how we came to be there, how we came to be here. We asked then to what extent battles were ongoing, what shape they took.

Warren passed along what she knew. "However the faces change," she said, "it's always the same blundering, mindless body beneath."

We were sitting out on what served as a café in Trace, the wraparound porch of a general store whose dry goods, groceries, staples of every sort, appeared for the most part to serve as barter. People came and went. Children played with pebbles, a jar and some small animal, a frog or lizard, in the shade of a sycamore.

Rain said to her, "You served."

"How could you tell?"

"Your language. Precise. Blunt."

"Two years. Went in when I was seventeen. Behind the lines, supply chains mostly, ordnance, but I saw enough."

"I'm sure you did."

"If I'd stayed longer, there wouldn't have been a choice to leave."

"I won't ask where," Rain said.

She met his eyes, nodded.

"You'd be welcome here," she said. "We have a couple of nurses who do what they can, one of them a midwife. No doctor for a long while. And now maybe we have two?"

She paused, just enough to check our reaction.

"I'm guessing you don't want to draw attention to yourselves, though. That could be a problem. If word got out. If you stayed on."

"We're a good distance from battle lines, right?" Rain said.

She nodded.

"Will anyone care where we're from?"

"Those outside Trace, you mean?"

"Assuming others hereabouts have similar needs, yes."

"Comes down to it being more a matter of actions than of origin, I'd think. Some are likely to believe you godsent."

"Oh?"

"The old religions have started taking hold again."

Rain turned to me. "So, in lives already abounding with surprise, it appears the two of us are about to become itinerant holy men."

Rain and I alone knew how that thought affected me, recalling as it did what I'd been told of my parents' flight from home.

MEMORY GOES ON ABOUT its work, stacking boxes of keepsakes atop one another, fully confident this is the stuff of a life. But memory's a poor historian, the keepsakes are bits and pieces that don't fit together. And life's a scatter.

We became part of Trace. Sequestered wasn't a word that came to us, but sequestered we were, knowing little of what transpired in the larger world. Upon occasion, from travelers passing through, we would hear that struggles for territory, truth, resources or influence indeed went on, but we could never parse the where and who of it. The country's many interior geometries, if never its transgressions, seemed ever-changing.

Through Suze Warren we met Liam Moore, direct descendant of the town's founder, Benjamin Trace. "Bit of a hermit," Suze said, the look of the cabin as we approached through woods supporting such, "and the town's shepherd." In what way the latter might we true we came but slowly to understand. Currents beneath a calm surface, we had to suppose at the time. The man we met that day had fine manners, as few words as possible for us and no evident interest in what went on beyond the clearing around his cabin.

One evening when we'd been in Trace close to a year, Rain, who'd taken to teaching at the local school, showed me a poem written by one of his students.

> It is April 27 in the Year of Confusion
> and the worst has not yet come.
> We have been expecting it
> for some time.

My friend longs for a land
where one isn't, as here, asked
where you came from
but where you'll go next.

We'd settled into place with little difficulty, Rain and myself. We cared for our neighbors, trekked out upon occasion to nearby towns to offer medical care, got down to the daily work of creating or recreating lives. Rain had discovered a flair for teaching older students, and I soon enough, if unwittingly, found myself entangled in town functions.

What Suze Warren said about old religions taking hold again proved true, not so much in Trace but in surrounding areas. As to this, Rain and I kept our own counsel, though I was never too far in thought from what Mother had described of the wreckage wrought back home in the self-proclaimed Year of Our Lord.

WEEKS AFTER SHARING HIS student's poem, Rain came to our house to tell us he'd be leaving soon. Hardly a surprise that his lifelong wanderlust would catch up with him—that, I'd expected—but it was a profound personal loss. I still opened doors expecting him to be there.

Again and again I find myself bogging down in my attempt to recreate those years. People in Trace went on about their work, tending crops, building and sewing and repairing, raising families, arguing, playing with jars and pebbles, burning trash, playing music, growing older, dying. One thing after another, then the same again, or most of it, none of it remarkable. What most lives are. And I a part of all that, for the first time.

Alison staggered into Trace much as Rain and I had. Just another stranger passing through, we all first thought. Exhaustion, hunger, thirst. A stranger to herself as much as to us, it turned out, for she could remember nothing of what brought her there, or of what came before. Memories trailed weeks behind. She had been taken from her home, she remembered that finally, taken by a group of older men, some of them had guns, she was sure of that, but she'd got away from them, then had no idea where she was and wandered, hoping someone would help her, till she came here. Where was she from? She didn't know, just the name of her town, which meant nothing to any of us. How long since she was taken? Months, she thought, but had no way of knowing. The moon kept changing, again and again.

By the time memories returned, she and I had begun growing close. Our makeshift hospital was a small building behind the café, once a storage facility. Alison remained there a week for hydration, mending and nourishment, then moved in with me.

Each home in Trace had an allotment of garden land at town's edge. Alison passed many of her mornings and afternoons at the allotment; we soon had a fine crop of herbs, zucchini and cherry tomatoes. Her mother always gardened, she told me, everything from sweet potatoes to green beans and kale. Alison didn't remember much about her father, who went off on business when she was five and never came back; she and her older brother were raised by their mom. She died when Alison was sixteen.

We had six years together. She couldn't bear children, but we felt no want, need or loss. Ours was a quiet life, of a kind I'd theretofore not believed possible, certainly not a kind I'd have believed myself party to, and one I might in younger days have mocked.

Alison worked beside me, ever attentive and a quick study, such that once Rain was gone she began caring for patients herself. Later, after attending a religious meeting with a former patient, she came into the habit of regular attendance and, by the same avenue of circumstance which brought her to medicine, began serving upon occasion as a lay cleric. As to that, as before, I kept my own counsel.

She was even then feeling the influence, if not consciously then otherwise, of the cancer that would take her. I'm fairly certain it was cancer. I was without X-ray capability, but Alison had all the proper signs and symptoms. Once the disease kicked in full force, its progression was mercifully quick.

THIS WAS ALL MANY years ago, little more left of any of it now, flickers of firelight against a wall, gusts of wind through fallen leaves. I stayed on, doing my work, taking up my space in town, as wars and ideologies exhausted one another, roads and trade reopened, nations found sure purchase and Trace began shape-changing. The population grew steadily as its youth headed off to other towns and other lives, and newcomers, many of these skilled workers or artisans, replaced them. Eventually, the town's medical needs well covered and with nothing to hold me there, I took my leave as well. A middle-aged man's walkabout. Some small part of Rain's rootlessness unrolling within me, perhaps.

I've done what I can here to hold these images, these times, in place.

Almost daily I remember what my mother told me of the kindness of the crossing guards and Mirela. And I think of the last two stories Rain told me.

One was a folk tale from ancient Scotland, about *wulvers* with the bodies of men and the heads of wolves, who came at night to leave fish on the windowsills of poor families.

The other is from just before he left Trace. Raised in church (he never said what kind), at age eleven he talked his entire school class—these were not religious people, mind you, they were the kids of farmers, factory workers, clerks—into publicly, all together, pledging their lives to the savior. We were sitting at the time near the sycamore where not long after our arrival, we'd watched children play. "You'd think that would make me feel good, right?" he said. "It didn't. It terrified me. That kind of power. I didn't want that, either the power itself or the obligations that come with it. I may have kept moving, all my life, because of that day."

I grew weary, myself, of obligations, of attachments. I'd never had, would never have, my uncle's fierce sense of rightness, Alison's or Mirela's kindness. We ache for our discontinuous lives to resolve into purposeful motion, straight lines, gain, coherence, but mine had no direction to it, neither away nor toward. That someone so undirected could inhabit so full a life remains to me a marvel and a mystery. I drifted, floated, reached out to take hold of what I could, for a while. How many of us, finally, do more?

TRACE, WHERE I CAME to rest, fell back to earth, swam to shore. Somewhere beneath it all, a suspicion of eternal returns: that those who struggle against destinies may only hasten them. We have this innate capacity to take the world we perceive, so large and diverse, and bend it to fit snugly around us, tucking in every corner. Rain, not long after we first met, holding up a hand: "Do we live in the world," then raising the other, "Or does the world live in us?"

With time, untraveled country roads, crumbling highways and newly opened trade routes all begin to look the same. Each horizon has a familiar face.

What do we imagine our coming back will comprise, then? The place to which we return can never be that which we left.

Trace, in these years of relative new plenty, was well on its way to becoming a modest city. The old general store long gone, a proper downtown had sprouted, complete with two-story buildings, six main streets on a grid, doctor's offices, lawyers, city hall, utility providers, multiple shops, a pharmacy, a women's center and two churches. Curiously, a replica of Liam Moore's cabin sat dead center on town square, not the actual one where "the town's shepherd" dwelt or hid out, but an exacting copy.

"He'd have hated it, the whole idea of it," Suze Warren said. She'd come across me early one morning as I sat with coffee from the corner café, looking over at the cabin. "I heard you were back. And keeping low."

"Getting on with life's about all I'm up for nowadays." She, on the other hand, gave off the same calm and confidence as when we'd first met, me a vagrant, she now in her late twenties. An older, more secure self. She'd become solidly just that. "You're not still running the show, I take it."

"Not for a long time. Hard to imagine who would want that, or if for some inscrutable reason they did, why on earth they'd admit it."

"Right, and right again."

"Ambition looks good on the young. Not so much later on, when it starts to wear you down with its own needs. But you don't have to give up what led you to ambition."

"Hopes for a better world?"

"One that's a little safer, a little less challenging, yes."

"That, or simple ego. Need for validation. Self-aggrandizement."

"On the list from day one."

"So what *is* it you do nowadays?"

"I teach. History, in what used to be called middle school. You?"

"Mostly it seems I sit in places like this and remember."

"Then we're doing the same work."

Pretty sure I smiled, at that. "I suppose in a way we are."

"You've seen a lot."

"And made sense of very little of it."

Suze had been standing the while. Now she sat by me on the bench.

"You're still a physician."

"Years and years since I practiced. And there are three already."

"You counted?"

"Just getting the lay of the land."

"I was thinking more . . . counseling? Younger folk, people who have difficulty interacting with others, that sort of thing."

"The country doesn't have enough problems as it is, you want to get all that started back up? Next thing you know, you've got life coaches, therapists and psychiatrists coming out of the woodwork."

"Good point. But so was mine. You'd be good at the work, and valuable."

There the brief tale of how, sitting on a bench one day in my fumbling, scruffish age, I became the guy who sits sounding out the burdens, terrors and misgivings of others day by slow day. Suze's use of *work* is what did it for me. So much of my life, early and late, had been the work I did. I'd always found some service, some project or occupation, to hold me in place, to *give* me a place.

I do, sometimes, still question to what degree my avocation as lay counselor can be thought of as valid community service and to what degree as gatekeeping for the status quo. Whole new constellations of new stories, at any rate, came to me. Soon I found myself entwined with the burgeoning city.

Seya, who many years ago with her four children

in tow fled a village under attack, traversing a desert, then a narrow passage through mountains, to arrive in Trace with two of the children still alive.

Or Ari with only vague memories of different faces above and beside him, different hands holding him, passing him along, the taste of different foods, but he was, he believes, taken care of, sometimes well, other times fitfully, even begrudgingly, in his own adulthood fostering child after child, dozens of them, year after year, in other towns and, finally, here in Trace.

Howard, press-ganged into service and on the night following the first battle deserting, bashing in the head of a regular soldier barely into his teen years who tried to stop him.

Herve, released after four years of imprisonment for protests in one seaside nation, making his way away from there as fast as, ill and enfeebled, he could, then begging and upon occasion thieving his way inland, never taking anything other than food, never more than just enough to keep going.

Juliet who retells her parents' stories of the world before, one of grand buildings, grand cities, a great, sprawling nation—all I have left of them now, she says, and what I have to pass on, to offer those who come after.

FOUR OR FIVE YEARS after I returned to Trace, along about the time that getting up and down and moving around began to require prior planning, Rain passed through—on his way somewhere else, of course. I talked him into staying a few days. Days became weeks, and before rambling again got the better of him, we had a chance to talk over the years since we'd last been together. My review was quickly done with; the detail and extravagance of his, predictably, took a bit longer.

He had gone back to sea as part of a crew with which he'd sailed long ago as a Free Marine, taking to land at a scatter of familiar ports and new ones. Fancied themselves pirates nowadays, he soon came to realize, and he wanted nothing of it. Briefly joined freedom fighters in one nascent South American country until, wounded, he left. Lived on the streets—"they called them streets at any rate, out of kindness, I suppose"—in another. In prison for a time there, surviving off daily hunks of bread and watery milk, roaches and what he could take from fellow prisoners. Tale after tale.

And some of that, he said, was true, or close enough to truth as not to matter.

For Rain, I believe, life was pure alchemy, the base stuff of it forever by some occult, innate wisdom transformed to a brighter substance.

The night before he left, Rain told one last story. Early in his maritime days, he said, he'd shipped out with a lapsed philosopher, a man who had departed his position at what was then a major university in order to experience—to taste it, he said, to feel it in his fingers—the actual, teeming world.

"And did he?" I asked.

"He did. Though what it may have meant to him in the end, I have no way of knowing. The ship docked in Puerto Rico, and after many a week of fine, far-ranging conversation, we went our separate ways. I do wonder. Did he go back, was that dose, that taste, enough, or did he reach further, want more? Did it end his life as a philosopher or make him a better one?"

At that point, all I could do was nod. There was for me a sudden charge in the room, a bite into the world's fabric, a recognition.

"It may be," Rain said, "that the only way we get through our lives is by imagining elsewheres and other times."

LIKE RAIN'S TALES, SOME of what I've written down here, part of this history, is true, or close enough to truth as not to matter. I can no longer divine one from the other any more accurately than can you, reading this. The land behind changes as we leave it. Our control of what gets recollected weakens with time and, even then, still must be sorted.

Never much taken with children, I find myself spending more and more time with them, caring for them as part-time pediatrician, playing with or perhaps more properly among them, Trace's universal adoptive grandfather. Every month or so I give talks—history, what else?—at the free college coming to life and form at town's edge. There, aware both of how little they know of the poem's circumstances and suspecting how much they may feel it in their hearts, I read from Cendrars's *Prose du Transsibérien et de la Petite Jehanne de France*. Another era, another nation that's worlds away now, a revolution there, the young woman beside him, steam rising from soldiers' wounds as the train passes by . . .

Are all wars, all revolutions, all our small daily lifetimes, year after year, the same?

Every few weeks, still, the older folks gather near Liam Moore's cabin on the square, wind gentle in the trees, children at play with pebbles and jars beneath, to tell their stories.

I am one of them.

RECONSTRUCTION

Upon silence our noise is superimposed and, with silence overcome, eternally expands.

—*On the Bayou with Ghost*

"I'll build a city," Shannon says, "a new city." She doesn't say she'll refurbish, renovate or reinhabit the shells of cities standing all about us—lately become the fashion—but speaks of building anew in the same tone of voice and with the same matter-of-factness as she does about so much else. That the wickeds' teeth will fall out. That the pure mind must remain uncluttered. That everything we know has a soft underbelly. That dinner is late.

So why this city thing, we ask, and why now?

"The land, time itself, speaks through me," Shannon says.

And so, I suppose, it did.

We were eight years old then, of course, infinitely wise, filled with the buoyant gases of youth, speaking in high, unnatural, often silly voices. Also the children of revolutions both chaotic and subtle. Like most children born in those years.

And the cities at any rate did get built, as they always do, so that today I sit in a beautifully maintained park on a fashionable bench watching groups of city folk come and go and admiring the birds that are slowly regaining ground here among us, albeit with history peering over my shoulder as always, history and myself alike wondering what will come of all this, how long will it last. In fairness I must acknowledge personal pride to be a third participant. Silently I pride myself on standing straight while others my age hobble about bent and bearing canes. And while upon occasion I'm unable to recall the name of a friend or the title of a favored book, I find pride in remembering the upheavals, shambles and reconstitutions that have occurred in my lifetime. That, in a sense, *are* my lifetime.

Again and again our parents told us that across the sea there were nations like our own, some of them indeed the way ours once was, vast and powerful beyond imagining. Our parents were right, we couldn't imagine such. Nor am I sure we believed them. Our own nation was again of a piece, yes, but struggling mightily to rise, stand straight and be about its business.

Though we learned this only later, after both she and

Father were gone, our mother had been city born and came from one of those far lands. This was never spoken of before us, and while we recognized that her speech was somehow different, it had always been so, she'd always been Mother, and at the time we had little if any sense of different languages and cultures. In the bottom of a trunk long stored away we discovered, when going through their things, a sheaf of old letters still in their envelopes. I don't believe we had seen letters before, only read of them. There was also a dull metallic device resembling a small, spoutless teapot, possibly a data or voice recorder or meant for visual capture, but we couldn't puzzle out what it did or how to engage it. Shannon, being Shannon, had to take it apart, and when she did, tiny circuits and what looked like leftover commas from someone's theme paper fell out.

Sprockets, Shannon said. Back then words, occasioned by circumstance or wholly unoccasioned, would fall into her mind, something about the sound or heft of them pleased her, and she'd say them over and over. *Sprocket. Sprocket.*

Many of the envelopes bore actual, wildly colorful stamps, from another country as we were soon to discover, the earliest of them from our mother to our father handwritten in an uncertain but courageous English. Three of the letters held images as well (Shannon supplied the word, *photographs*): Mother in her late teens, standing on a mound of earth with water, a lake or pond, behind; Mother addressing a lecture hall filled with what we took to be students; Mother standing by a sculpture in, presumably, a museum.

"It appears our mother was a mail-order bride," Shannon said.

By the time we came upon the letters, Shannon was no longer saying words over and over, she barely spoke at all, such that so full and grammatical a sentence was remarkable. It had come to feel to me as though she resided in another world and was but a visitor hereabouts, dropping in from time to time to see what if anything had changed.

IT'S BECOME MY HABIT of late to pick up lunch at one or another of the market stalls, a sandwich, kabob or bowl of noodles, and carry the food with me down to the piers, watching the drift of barges southward as I eat, one of those commonplace rituals, meaningless in and of themselves, that have the power to hold our lives together, to give them shape.

I'd come from there back up into the park and taken a bench near the street. Few others were about in the park itself; beyond, the street bustled. Delegates from one of the new East European nations are visiting the city today, ostensibly to negotiate new trade agreements (for what, the media fails to mention), and preparations are everywhere. Crews have been out all week rounding up the homeless to cart them off to ballrooms, schoolhouse gyms and meeting halls temporarily repurposed as shelters, hauling away barrels of trash and the otherwise unseemly, carrying out a general, makeshift reinvention. In some stray recess of our collective mind we still long to be kinder, gentler, more kempt beings.

As I'm thinking this, one of the new militia vehicles cruises slowly by. These hit the streets about a year ago, supposed not to look like an official van at all, meant to move about incognito—*passing*, as it were—but the tires give them away. Ectomorph above, mesomorph beneath. You have to wonder how many engineers and committees it took to come up with this, and why none of them took note. Jokes abound.

On the far side of the park, down by the bridge, a school marching band is practicing, perhaps to take part in some parade or function having to do with our East European visitors? Too many clarinets and drums, at any rate, and far too little agreement as to what might constitute correct pitch.

My apartment's in a distant part of the city, an older section whose loss of structural integrity has only increased its charm. Usually I hop the train, once in a great while splurge and take a water taxi back to one of the landings nearby, mostly I walk.

Walking invigorates, loosens old joints and muscles, promotes deep breaths and brings old friends together, city and self, to become reacquainted. My neighbor Padma would say it allows one behind the curtain to see how the magic actually happens. But I suspect that whatever magic may once have been here is long gone—from the city itself, or from this viewer's eye. I do remain surprised that however much it changes, parts of it in decay, other parts reborn, people moving in and out and around, the city still can feel inherently so much the same.

Padma's a journalist. Months back, when she was writing a piece about old-world filmmakers she showed me opening frames from a Soviet-era movie and without conscious thought I blurted out "That's *my* place!" Everything gray and grainy and somehow looking not quite fully formed, doorways right and left that appeared to lead to more of the same, battered pots and pans on the counter, two chairs and a sorely used table.

The uncluttered life, Shannon would say. Leading to an uncluttered mind. But my mind is anything but uncluttered.

Home in my very own gray and grainy, I pull up Gynn's book-length poem about the Nation Wars, press on a page or two from where I'd stopped before only to stop again. This isn't a book to be approached with anything less than full attention. Next I have a go at a classic Blaze novel, set during the first Union Day celebrations in a world so different from our own that for all its cleaving to classic genre structure the book now reads every bit as much a fantasy as it does an historical mystery. By the time the first missing person shows up, page sixteen, I've gone missing as well. I put the link on standby. The wink of its tiny green light assures me it will be ready again when I am.

The wandering mind is far less tethered.

State feeds overflow with preparations for, clips of or heads discussing the visiting delegation. Local sites look elsewhere, to essay-like surveys of city neighborhoods, brief documentaries of charitable and non-profit groups, thumbnails of the husbands, wives, offspring, associates and colleagues of those making, defending and interpreting our laws.

All much the same.

But the locals also keep tabs on protestors who, silent and orderly, turn up of a sudden in small groups near the capitol, draw militia to themselves, then quietly disperse as another group surfaces in the distance, their movements in, out and about, the sureness and grace of it all, suggesting, rather than *tactical*, the descriptor *choreographed*. Better than half the protestors look to be of an age such as to remember, like myself, the late swells of the Union Wars.

My father was born in one of the first of the new

cities, a city not so much built as autonomously grown: settlement, village, town, city. Every few days there, Father said, a man everyone called Doc would join a gathering of elders on the town square to speak of their lives. They all had good stories but, because he'd traveled widely and seen so much in his life, Doc's stories were the best. Before long, others started retelling them. How he took care of the dying and wounded from both sides of battles. How he'd taken as his wife another refugee like himself only to lose her to illness. How in his final years he found his way to easing troubled minds and served as physician to the town's children. Doc had been all his life a healer and, with him gone, Father said, his stories had gone on healing.

I roll slowly through update sites. Protestors, the dedication of a new city library, protestors again, new military spending bill poised to pass without hitch, legal battles over the Jump procedure continue. Somewhere in the mix, a song from Salya, her first recording in a decade.

> Let me tell you
> what I know,
> this won't take long:
> It all goes away,
> it all goes away

—

WHEN SHE'S FOURTEEN SHANNON will say:

Soon I'll be shot to death by the soldiers of god.

Half a century from now, as a society we'll drain the blood of others, the weak, the powerless, to replenish communal water supplies.

Nothing, not even salvation, lasts. In the blink of an eye, with a single shot, it's lost.

She will say these are things she has read in books, and they are true.

PADMA'S FRIEND MILAN, A doctor, has gone back to university to become a lawyer. He was, or is, a surgeon—by definition, one would think, an activist who at heart must believe that damage, fault or impairment can be set right. Does this carry over to his pursuit of the law? I once asked a tactful version of that question, his response being that he has no fantasy of coming thereby to understand how society works and certainly none as to how it might be repaired. Finally, he said, his new agenda has more to do with trying to understand how we fool ourselves into believing there's order in a society, then fool ourselves again into thinking we can restore it.

That same day, I asked what it was like for him going back to school, slipsliding as a professional from one demanding occupation to another. In response he spoke with a devotee's passion of early television in the old world—sitcoms, talent contests, reality shows—suggesting that his day-to-day could well be rich fodder for any one of those, or all.

We'd been on our way, Padma, Milan and myself, to check out for ourselves the city's proud new feature, a building designed by architect J. Feather for the city's university. Like so much of the city, the university campus had grown fast and waywardly, with little time set aside for planning. Navigating it proved quite the challenge. We struck out confidently, strayed, wandered about then retraced our steps repeatedly before stopping to hail a passing student, and had scarcely begun our query when she said, "The Feather, right? Of course. Turn left there"—She indicated an older, stately three-story building—"then follow the path between two quonsets behind. You'll come onto a common with plots of flowers, a square stone fountain. Go straight on through the common and there you are."

Talk of the town it was, Milan had told us, and one could see why. He pointed to a tunnel-like ramp emerging from the structure's vitals only to sink to a dead end near the top of a low wall.

"That was to be straight, as by the entryway, running right through the building—like the notion of a Klein bottle, inside and outside joined. That's what Feather intended. So it's all glass, open to view. But when the builders got around to it they found they didn't have the space. This is what they came up with."

"The brute power of nonimagination," Padma said.

"With insult added to injury. This was commissioned to be the fine arts building. Now administration won't let students paint in it for fear of its getting all messy, irksome and disfigured. With smears and stains on the floors and such, you know."

Padma: "Can't have ugly spoil the beauty."

Milan: "The great unforeseen."

"So they set up the quonsets behind Old Main," Padma said.

"For studios, yes. And now they want funding to put up a second building for fine arts, a replacement. It's a major case study at school—lawyers have been punching this out for years, almost from the time ground first got broken. Allegations as to misuse of funding, frozen accounts and appeals on same, stacks of unpaid invoices, multiple breaches of contract . . . on and on."

Afterward we went for refreshments to a café just off campus where we might have been parents and in my case grandparent to any others present. Over tapas-size plates of hummus, soft cheese, bits of smoked meats and pickled vegetables, we sat for some time drinking from generous mugs of coffee or tea and speaking of the building, then of the protestors beginning to appear with greater frequency and presence. At length we'd moved on to other matters, some less urbane, others more so, when Padma spoke up: "Change is a light glimpsed in distant windows. Some can't help but walk toward those windows. Others turn their eyes away."

"Classic Padma! Even to the timing!" Milan said, laughing. Then, to me: "You'll see it soon on her stack. Or in the book of such sayings I've long suspected her to be assembling."

"To help others on their way?"

"I rarely know what I think," Padma said, "until I write or speak it."

FOLLOWING LUNCH, MY ATTEMPT at reading and my slow-moving scan online, my dance card goes empty. Not that I have a dance card. Time lies out ahead, flat to the horizon, boon and bane wearing the same face. The sort of day, perhaps, that calls out for old films. Those that seem somehow to be shot black and white even when not. Where wind batters at windows as the rain takes back everything it has lost.

It's perpetually fascinating what one could get accomplished with a couple of cameras the size of small tanks, some overcast sky, shots of deserted streets, rain on a window, a handful of ill-fitting baggy suits and a sharp dress or three. And hats—don't forget the hats. Great hats, men and women alike. This one had them all, from slouch hats for the guys at the newsstand or driving taxis, to uniform hats for postmen, police and military, to some truly fine fedoras and a handsome straw or two. Partway in, as well, I started wondering why no one has put together what they used to call a coffee-table book with photographs documenting women's fashionable eyebrows through the years.

The movie itself was adamantly of its kind, people coming and going again and again from apartments, shops, cars, stairs and doorways, long pulls of traffic and skyline, gunshots suddenly ringing out as they did back then, a detective stomping about the penthouse saying, "Bullet through the chest, ma'am. Just routine."

Following that welcome recess having little enough to do with art and still less with actual life—instantly disposable yet in its own rude way regenerative—I find myself back at the piers, water being a primal restorative.

I'm looking out at boats moving slowly, timelessly it seemed, on the water, much as one peers into aquariums, not so much watching as having in a sense entered to dwell there for a moment, suspended, floating, free. But I'm thinking of something quite different.

I came awake of a sudden (alive again, I might say) to searing light and violent washes of sound with absolutely no understanding of where I was, why or who—knowing only flood upon flood of pain, fear and alarm, the hell-bent urge to flee, to get away at any cost. And couldn't. No part of my body would respond, head, trunk, arm, leg. I could see only the pockmarked white ceiling above, where, in one broken corner of the overhead light, a spider had built its web.

Years later I'd learn of Tolstoy in the years following what he spoke of as his vastation, when he glimpsed the great spaces of the world and his own insignificant place within, coming thereby to recognize the aristocracy of which he was a part as a crushing burden on all others, to become for the remainder of his life a Christian pacifist and anarchist, founding schools for the children of peasants liberated in 1861, going so far as to dress himself in peasant clothing to identify with them, and I would wonder if this waking without sense or knowledge of self might have been *my* vastation.

Alas, no. Of a sudden, in yet another flood, it all came back. The scream of a shell incoming, the ringing deafness following impact, everything around us overturned, upended, screen of the world gone dark from smoke and debris.

Pain.

Then nothing.

"You are going to be okay, sir."

A voice beside me, to my right. A man's face moved in to occlude my spider and its light fixture. Young. My age, or close to it? Vision blurred, unsure.

"You'll soon enough be moving about, sir. It's the drugs."

Jacob went off and fetched a doctor back to my bedside, a spindly man with hair like copper shavings who (as I would later learn) rarely quite met one's eyes. He introduced himself as Dr. Sobin and explained that until the evening before I had been kept in an induced coma. To help in the healing, he said. And not to worry over the paralysis, in a few hours it would pass.

We'd been sent forth, Billy Dan, Lev and myself, to locate and scavenge food. Billy Dan was a genial young man, strong, capable and loyal, whose tongue seemed always to be slightly protruding from his mouth, Lev a boy harboring no enmity toward the world or any other within it, who had simply found himself in that place and time and done his best. The larger mission was against a group of towns lying to our west and a shade north, from which raiders spread throughout the region, thieving supplies, weapons, water, whatever came or might be made available. Two weeks back, under cover of night, one of their parties had broken into our common house and carted off virtually all our food stocks.

They may have considered their alliance of towns

to be an upcoming nation and themselves soldiers in the cause. We thought of ourselves as the same, yet mostly as a group of people trying to stay alive, a community collectively driven to survive. But that is just as likely how the others started off thinking. Now, to survive, we had to find food. And to go on surviving, one way or another, overtly or covertly, we would have to act as they did.

Dr. Sobin listened to heart, lungs and bowel, thumped about my chest and neck, tugged for a moment at what must have been sutures or bound wounds, then left. I asked Jacob how long I'd been out. Close on to four weeks, he said. Much of the initial week back and forth to surgery and procedures. Before which, you became a member of the club.

Club?

"Of the recently dead. Not so exclusive as it sounds. Scraped you off the windshield's what we'd say back as field medics. But they managed to get everything stapled, fused, bolted, sewn or glued back more or less where it ought to be. Put in the time, it should all work again."

I asked about Billy Dan and Lev. Jacob told me what he'd heard. One died trying to haul me to safety. So far they'd found no trace of the other.

I was twenty-four then, halfway into a decade of infantry and patrol. I can't tell anymore, of those or later issue, which scars are which. Memories, too, are interwoven, a patchwork.

One of the smaller boats, no more than fifteen feet bow to stern perhaps, appears to be having trouble, liquid blossoming in the water around it. Something they were carrying as cargo? Oil? Fuel? Two men on deck are shouting and moving rapidly about as the boat begins nosing toward the pier just downriver. Upriver, two guards exit the watch station, climb aboard a scout and pull onto the water heading this way.

I walk back through the park, thoughts veering from ancient pirate movies filled with buckle-swashing, to idle wonder at how the conference is proceeding, to, again, that first hospital stay, where I spent more time with my paired physical and occupational therapists, hours, days, weeks, than I'd ever spent with anyone. Both of them slender, wiry, hair cut short, narrow faces. In actuality they may not have resembled one another as closely as it seems; in memory they do.

Ever surprising how much we take for granted. Walking. Standing. Being able to reach for something, to grasp it. To dress oneself. How much effort and coordination these minimal activities require. The degree of concentration necessary, such that the need blocks out all surroundings. As with a terrible slowness you relearn. As body and mind come to a new truce.

Set was a refugee from one of the far west cities. He'd been medic there and one day, after providing first aid to a gunshot victim lying in the street, a young man like himself in his early twenties, he had stood, stepped away and kept going. Crossed much of the continent on foot, arriving with clothes he'd taken off someone's porch clothesline when his own grew too sweat-soaked and crusty to wear.

Kelsey was perhaps fifteen years older and had passed through any number of occupations, elder caretaker, teacher, information tech, before coming onto the one that held firm. If you watched closely you could see the brief hitch when her left arm came into play, the aftermath of a worksite bombing as it happens, and might surmise this was how she'd arrived at her current profession.

Both were open, affable, dedicated. Kelsey and Set worked me mercilessly and, as I staggered between handrails or lay on my back sending unrequited instructions to legs, we talked. They told me about their lives, I spoke of mine, something I'd rarely done before. Our efforts became, for me, much more than simple repair.

The world had slid and tilted strangely away from me. Strolling hallways on my walker, I could look only down to my feet; if I glanced to the side or further ahead, whatever frail hold I had on equilibrium vanished. Coming into any open space, emerging even from my room, dizziness and muscle weakness crashed onto me, a physical wash of panic for which the team's *vertigo* seemed comically inadequate. At any moment I would fall. Everything in the world about me, everything, shook and shivered and shifted. I couldn't distinguish the ebb and flow of the room's ventilation from my own heartbeat.

Kelsey and Set taught me work-arounds and urged me through my paces till these had become second nature, then took them away, moved others into place and we started up anew. New challenges, new bridges, new paths. Four months later I was back in country. Six weeks after that, again in hospital. Then came out to find our small part of the world at a frangible peace.

WHEN I WAS RECOVERING, that first time, at some point during each night I'd look up to see Shannon standing by the door to my room. She wouldn't come in, and by then had completely stopped speaking. Nothing showed on her face. There was no affect at all. She rarely ate.

I learned not to approach or to speak when she showed up, but to sit on the side of the bed and meet her eyes. This seemed (though admittedly it may have been nothing more than my own self-serving fancy) to calm her. She'd remain there, four minutes, six, lights from outside upon occasion gliding down her body, shadowing the wall behind, then step away.

For those minutes she was as enigmatic, as frozen in time—no, as outside time, untouched by it—as women in early de Chirico paintings. The frame of my door, the backstop of wall, became one with the deserted squares and shadowy arcades of those paintings, their women without features, their unending afternoons.

De Chirico.

That's Dr. Ben, speaking through me. He loved the goofiness of surrealists, to whom he introduced me. The first time we met he told me he'd just that morning decided that *Here I Lie* would do double duty as the epitaph on his tombstone and the title of his autobiography. Ben was a friend of Set's, ever sharply dressed, even in scrubs somehow, and at the least provocation or with none at all on the verge, so it seemed, of breaking into slapstick song and dance.

"Hey, best thing in the world for your rehab," Set said when he learned of Ben's and my relationship—short-term, as it happened. We'd barely figured out countermeasures for my disabilities and pain when Ben volunteered. "For the life of me—mark those words—I cannot recall doing so," he said at the time. He was posted to a field hospital at (again his words) "the absolute ass end of the front."

Traffic's slow on the river today, small boats mostly,

water rolling so lazily to either side that the word *drifting* comes to mind. Peaceful here, as always.

This, by water, is how Ben came back, his container stacked sideways with others in the hold of a government ship, draped in the nation's new flag.

My second recovery gig went multiple choice: Believed lost behind enemy lines (where the lines were, how could one tell?) pronounced MIA (no doubt about that), and finally (correct answer) he who emerges from near death having survived on bark, insects and stolen mouthfuls of domestic animal food.

Free of that adventure and once again badly wounded, down sixty pounds with impressively reduced muscle mass, mostly I remember lying on my bed in pools of sweat that smelled vaguely of brine, bad meat and sewage, with people hovering above to tell me what, from the cant of their voices and fixed expressions, had to be important information. But the slow crawl of light across the ceiling, the muffled bleat of horns and alarms sounding as though from aboard some phantom ship, were of far greater interest.

That second recovery, Shannon didn't come to stand by my door. By then she had completely given up speaking and all personal interaction, and was sheltered in an extended-care facility upstate, Mallard Home. Actually it was nice there, my parents told me. She had her own room, she and a roommate a few years older, and there were activities, regular therapy sessions, courses of all sorts offered, including college-level, though Shannon admittedly took no part in any of that.

From the moment such became possible, I made it my habit to travel upstate each week, three hours up, three back, to visit my sister. We'd sit side by side in a dayroom watching old movies and older TV shows, her features so unchanging that I had to wonder what if anything got through, or again side by side in chairs out on the well-kept lawn, she straight in the chair barely moving at all, myself steadily shifting and fidgeting in the attempt to ease bones and joints too long overwrought.

Eight weeks in, she turned to me in the dayroom during an episode of *The Pretender* and said *You've brought memory's bones with you.* Nothing more after that, week after week, till late one evening as I accompanied her back to her room, rushing so as not to miss the last train home, she spoke again: "I can see it in your eyes, what Yeats saw, new worlds flowing in to take the place of the old. Caesar, Cleopatra. Yours like theirs, a mind moving upon silence."

The last words from her I would hear.

That was the day of our field trip. I'd applied for a pass and, when to my surprise it was granted, Shannon and I attended a performance of flamenco dancing at the city art museum. A man, a woman, a guitarist on stage. The woman danced first, in bold, joyous movements, taking over the small stage, filling it, enfolding the audience in her brightness, her vitality. Respectfully, solidly formal, the man took his turn only to be rejected by her, whereupon he retreated far stage left and came almost to a full stop, a single foot still in motion, tapping lightly, barely at all, toe to heel. Then with a wrenching, all but unbearable slowness the foot grew active, fully alive, the other joined in, and the man was again dancing full out, moving back to stage center, more powerful, more assured, more joyful with each step, the guitarist echoing his every sound, every movement, every cadence. At that moment I turned to Shannon and saw the tears running down her face.

SIX MONTHS FURTHER ALONG I was no longer to be a part of whatever wars we might become engaged in, therapeutic short walks had become workaday recreative ones and, that very morning, I'd hosted my first halting run, upon return from which I found visitors waiting, as they say, on my stoop.

There were two, Doctors Robert Huang, Chief of Special Services at Union Memorial Hospital, and Valery Mason.

Dr. Mason's scraggly beard and indifferent clothing, by intent, I believe, gave off an air of someone quite older, suggesting to me a man who might doubly harbor self-assurance and self-doubt. The slant of his opening remarks appended a suspicion that he was of the type who, before committing, firmly believes he has weighed every conceivable alternative.

Dr. Huang came across more as gatekeeper than player, nothing much of the world savior in his eyes, possibly a man for whom, one way or another, in the end everything came to a balance.

It took some time for the dust jacket and front matter to tick down to readable pages, the pith and gist of which was this.

The two of them, I should understand, while primarily affiliated with Union Memorial, worked as well with Mallard Home, where my sister resided. True, they had no involvement with the facility's everyday functions, daily care and maintenance and such, but they did serve as consultants. Furthermore, for almost two decades now they'd jointly overseen multiple research projects, first largely at their own and Union Memorial's expense, more recently with government funding and *most* recently had come to focus on a single project.

How much do you know, Dr. Mason asked, of Doctor Szasz's work with augmenting the nervous system?

I'd heard old men's tales of soldiers with jacked-up senses and superhuman abilities—we all had—and assumed they were just that, tall tales. Such was not the case, Dr. Mason told me. The stories were true, those soldiers were real and the so-called Jump procedure derived from Szasz's breakthroughs.

This was years ago, at the beginning of the second Nation War, Dr. Mason continued. The Jump was problematic from the first and had remained so, as evident from cases still before various courts—seemingly endless—concerning ownership of the procedure, use of same, control of same. Backing up, though, taking the longer view, what Szasz had developed was wildly innovative, brilliantly original. It was also, Dr. Mason assured me, generative. Szasz's work had given us the map, he said. A map to reset, to rebuild, entire nervous systems.

Knowledge of my sister's situation came to their attention at precisely the right time. Her debilities fell directly in line with the objective of Dr. Mason's project. Psychologists supposed that Shannon's nervous system had become hypersensitive, perhaps even originated so, and in response had for years been shutting down, bit by bit. Dr. Mason believed they were wrong, that what the psychologists were seeing was, so to speak, a corruption of the operating system, defaults that could be identified, located and overwritten.

I can go in, he said. I can pin the map, I can rebuild.

OUR VISIT FROM THE East European delegates appears to have ended with no declaration of new policies or accommodations forthcoming but without any major hustle, upset or boondoggle as well, which is likely the best we can hope for given the tenor of the time, theirs a new nation, ours newly awakening, much of the rest of the world biding its time.

News of that world onlink today includes what appear to be beachheads of a new religion in parts of provincial China (*beachheads* being the very word used), temporary lockdowns in major German cities after widespread riots to challenge recent elections, reports of renewed drone attacks across west Saudi borders. The usual stream of hostilities, battles, deployments at one site and, a click or two up or down, all-too-familiar peace talks, cease fires and that-a-boys for groups struggling to feed troubled regions, provide emergency medical care, offer relocation support.

I put out my finger, push and the world, that world, goes away.

Wind has come up strong today, August 18, the day in 1936 that Federico Lorca was shot to death by Nationalists at Fuente Grande, Great Spring. Ancient history. But rivers still run, winds rise and fall, those who believe they own the world remain restless, anxious, driven. Here in this old part of a new city, doors no longer fit frames, nor windows theirs; through them I feel the breath of those winds.

It's with me in the park as well, rummaging trees, as I pass through on the way home from second Tuesday dinner with old friends at Fio's, an inner-city bar and grill dressed down to a mock-up of rural pubs. We've been getting together like this for at least a year, eight or ten regulars, you never know who'll show up. The only thing that's sure are two rules: no exchange of complaints about growing old, what hurts most today or the latest physical breakdown; no talk of politics past, present or future.

With official posturing now over, frequent outages are back, power and lights holding for the time being in the central city, uncertain elsewhere. The park is slowly returning to life. Walkers, bikers, a few families with children. The recently evicted homeless are filtering back to rebuild their encampments in and around the park. Two meters off the walk, passersby have gathered around baby birds—blown from their tree by the wind, I assume. A woman is gingerly transferring them one by one to the hollow of her palm.

The others had arrived before me and were already well into the thicket of drinks and chatter.

Marek was among the city's major planners for eighteen years before his retirement, which, he said, "more closely resembled a surrender." Billie, a legal secretary, has for her entire freelance career declined, "for reasons of personal freedom and distaste at becoming any further a part of the system," every offer of permanent employment. Jeb's a quartermaster turned truck driver turned EMT turned animal-rescue veterinarian who claims he's turned around so much that "sideways, I kinda disappear." Heedlessly cheerful Sylvie is still considered one of the nation's top photographers though it's been more than a decade since she worked, the truth of the thing being, she says, that "some unspoken agreement seems to have come about, cease and desist all this bother and I'd be rewarded."

I said hello to all, accepted the menu the waiter offered while swearing I'd order something different this time then asked for my usual shepherd's pie, prompting such fulsome laughter from tablemates that others in Fio's turned to look.

We chatted at formless this-and-thats. I told Jeb about the baby birds, witnessed what I'd seen as to park and city coming back to normal, use of the word *normal* predictably bringing on a round of sarcasm to match the previous laughter. Before long, with a comment by Sylvie, I sensed the conversation trending future tense.

"What I mean is," she continued, "is there any chance we'd even recognize the world our grandchildren will grow up in?"

I pushed in to remark that we'd gone seriously off script, that what old farts like us are expected to do is just get together and talk about the past. Not the future—the past. Old times. What we remember, what we're able to remember, about them.

Freshly returned from getting us all new drinks or coffee and catching what I said, Jeb countered: "Which may be one reason old farts doze off so much."

My pitiable effort to pull us back on track gone belly up.

Today's topic, like it or not: the nation as it stands, how stable is it.

"WE ARE SORRY," DR. Mason told me. A damnably beautiful day outside. Through the window behind him I watched an adolescent walking her small dog, a terrier, I think. "Certainly not the success we'd hoped for—nor was it by any means a failure," he said, this deep-thinker unbound as are most of us by the simplistic binary of A or non-A.

The intensity of sunlight on the wall, the angle at which it falls. The girl's attraction to her dog. The correlation between the length of the shadows they throw, the position of the sun overhead and the time of day. Everything has an explanation. Everything is knowable.

"You keep saying that, she is so much better. But why? On what grounds do you claim to know?"

"You've only to look. Your sister attends to all her

own needs. She moves without hesitation or confusion through her day. Truth is what we see."

"Partly—and partly what we imagine."

I've no idea how many iterations of this dialogue took place. Four, eight, twelve? Dr. Mason insisting that Shannon could now have, even that she had, a normal life (*normal* as always a word deserving mistrust), hitting that monotonous beat again and again like a child with its first toy drum. My sister was self-dependent, yes, but she'd never truly been less, and still she refused to speak, related to no one, acknowledged another's presence, if at all, only with the slightest smile.

From Mallard Home, Shannon moved to a halfway house, Fauci Center, where I visited her each day. I brought fresh croissants or donuts still warm in their paper sack and we'd sit outside in warm sunlight if such was to be had; if not, in the common room of muted browns and shaded windows as other residents came and went; or in her room—it made no seeming difference to her—watching TV shows onlink. I soon found that nature shows unfailingly brought on the smile. (I would say "calmed her," but calm was her default.) This was true even of shows inherently violent, with lions dragging an elk carcass across the tundra, crocodiles lunging from the water to take down zebras, reptile parents eating their own offspring, Alaskan-bear mother and cub tearing into a freshly caught salmon.

We can't ever know what goes on in another's mind, of course, what the world we supposedly share looks like from in there. In Shannon's case, this bifurcation exceeded mere distinctions of perspective or interpretation; hers seemed not at all the same world. As I'd sensed long before, it was as though she dwelled elsewhere.

Our last visit, years and years ago, fell this month, August 24. That was the day Simone Weil died in the sanitorium at Grosvenor Hall in Kent, age thirty-four, laid low by frailness and abiding ill health, refusing to eat perhaps as a reflection of her personal take on Christian mysticism, perhaps from denial of self and solidarity with the suffering of her countrymen in occupied France.

And with these memories, of Weil, of Shannon, I have to wonder, as often before: Does history truly serve to help us understand, to ferret out unseen lines of action and influence, lines that connect all of us one to another, and to render the disorder we perceive in the world about us to workable patterns? Or is it possible, likely even, that these lines we believe we discover, and the maps we make from them, are little more than illusion?

Shannon and I had passed much of that clear blue day outside beneath trees, bolstered by a plate of the oily sardines that were among her favorites, mustard on the side for dipping. I can't remember when or how I discovered that combination. With day recumbent in the hills, I'd got her settled back in her room and packed up to leave. As I went over to kiss her goodbye, she removed a small piece of paper from the pocket of her denim shirt and held it out to me, smiling, the last time I'd see that smile. There, in long-unpracticed handwriting, the conclusion of a poem by Langston Hughes.

> I see the island,
> And its sands are fair.
> Wave of sorrow,
> Take me there.

The bus ride home was just over an hour, darkness shouldering slyly in around. In the seat across from me, a young mother and son sat silently, looking out the window. Everyone aboard, it seemed, was doing the same, as though everywhere, the world over, we all sat waiting.

When Shannon and I were young, before we encountered it in schoolbooks, our parents told us about Martin Luther King and the speech he'd made over a hundred years earlier, saying he had a dream. As do we all? Some we broadcast, some we pretend at, some we never speak, never voice even to ourselves. Dreams are imagings, supposings, aspirations: thin air by the time they reach ground.

The following day, the administrator at Fauci Center called to inform me that Shannon was missing. She'd left sometime during the night, personal effects and clothing in the single small duffel bag she arrived with. Despite every attempt, in all these years since, she has never been found, never again been heard from.

My dream? A world in which all are equal not only by law but in opportunity as well, a world in which governing agencies strive to protect the vulnerable and help us all rein in our basest instincts, in which empathy supplants greed and limits suffering and together we become a true commonwealth where acquisition and ever-increasing wealth are never again so loud an engine as to block out the sound of all others. I dream that.

Wave of sorrow, take me there.

Take us all.